APPLE OF FATE

A GODS AMONG US NOVELLA

ELLE BEAUMONT

Midnight Tide
PUBLISHING

Apple of Fate
Copyright © 2021 by Elle Beaumont

Published by Midnight Tide Publishing.
www.midnighttidepublishing.com
Cover designed by Harvest Moon Designs
facebook.com/groups/HarvestMoonDesigns
Edited by Meg Dailey
thedaileyeditor.wordpress.com/editing-services

ELLE BEAUMONT

APPLE OF FATE

CONTENTS

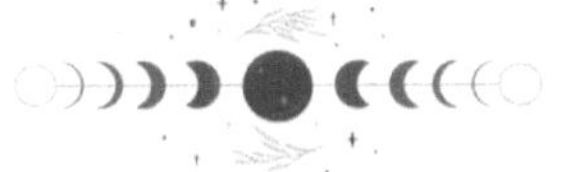

*Kendel, this one is for our insta-love relationship.
One week on the beach with you was enough to send me head
over heels into our happily ever after.*

Acontius

2019
Modern Day Ephesus
Selçuk, Turkey

Tourists milled around the dirt pathway in front of the temple's ruins. There wasn't much left of Artemis' temple, which had been rebuilt thrice in the past thousands of years. Eventually, patrons gave up and said it was the will of the gods that the temple remain in ruins. It wasn't. Acontius had listened to the goddess curse the names of her patrons as they forgot her and called her a myth and no more.

A myth couldn't bring a mortal to their knees.

At a young age, Acontius had witnessed what Artemis was capable of: love, wrath, vengeance. She'd saved him from death once as a plague swept through his home island, raised him as one of her own, and in return, she asked for his service, his allegiance. Which he'd given her freely as a boy, but after centuries of being alone, he wanted *more*.

Day in and day out, he watched as families strolled through the old sacred grounds. Children laughing, couples leaning in together as they took pictures. Acontius wanted that.

Acontius pulled an apple from a brown paper bag, buffing the golden skin on the lapel of his black sports jacket. He sighed, raising the apple to his mouth, just as he caught sight of one tourist venting to her companion.

"I don't want to be stuck behind the newlywed couple," the female tourist muttered. "Because, yes, I'm still getting over Matt." She spun away from the sight of the ruins, her chestnut hair woven into a crown braid. Luminous brown eyes caught ahold of his hazel pair for a moment, and in that instant, Acontius saw what he often felt churning inside him: loneliness. But as quickly as their eyes met, her father (he guessed, judging by their similar facial structure) pulled her back toward the site.

In recent years, Acontius' immortality had gnawed at him. But it was more than that; it was the fact that he'd taken a vow to remain untethered. After thousands of years alone, he finally wanted what he couldn't have: a life with one he loved.

Twisting his lips, he plucked a pen from his pocket and stared down at the apple in his hand. With little thought, he etched words into the skin of the fruit.

A voice up the pathway called out to the group. "We are

about to continue speaking, please join us if you don't want to miss out."

The woman that had caught his attention didn't budge. The man she was with shrugged and continued on, muttering something Acontius couldn't hear.

She turned, facing the ruins. A pile of stone rubble, a lone column, and a sad pool of water that had once been a great pond.

Idly, Acontius wondered what she saw beyond the ruins.

He couldn't think about it for too long. This was his moment. Now or never.

Rolling the apple toward the young woman's feet, he quickly dodged out of her line of sight.

The apple rolled until it nudged her foot. She yelped in surprise and bent down, inspecting it as if it were from an alien planet. She spun it around until the etched surface stared up at her, and in disbelief, she recited the words. "I swear by Artemis to marry Acontius." She squinted at the apple, scoffing before she tossed it down the hill.

Acontius' heart thundered in his ears. She had no idea the weight her words held, or what a vow meant on sacred ground.

What had he done in that foolish moment?

Artemis would have his immortality, and then hunt him down when she found out. But then, why did he grin? Why did his eyes light with pure joy?

That young woman had made a vow on sacred ground, which meant one thing: it'd have to come to fruition.

Delia

Present Day
West Palm Beach, Florida

Delia's nails clacked away at her laptop's keyboard as she updated her resume. In the past six months, she'd managed to not only lose her job but also her relationship with her long-term boyfriend. 2020 was not looking to be her year like she'd claimed it would be.

She groaned.

The doctors had been puzzled over what caused her hospitalizations. Each time she'd collapsed, unresponsive, and her blood test results tanked, showing her organs about to fail. It was the third time she had been admitted to the hospital when they deemed it a possibility she was doing this to herself.

Why, in heaven's name, would she send herself to the hospital in such a state?

They claimed it was for attention.

Delia claimed something was wrong with her.

And that was how, and why, her last boyfriend, Jacob, dumped her. And why her boss suggested an extended leave of absence, which was another term for, "We don't want to fire you, but you also can't work here."

Jacob had concluded she was harming herself, either by prescription drugs or something else, and when she denied it —because it wasn't true—he left. It hurt, but she didn't need someone like that in her life. What stung more was losing her job. It was the icing on top of the cake.

Amidst her typing, her phone blared "Waiting for Superman" by Daughtry. She snatched it up and peered at the screen. A picture from last year's trip to Greece and Turkey stared at her. She and her father stood in front of the remains of the Temple of Artemis in Selçuk.

She frowned at the screen, then answered. "Hey, Dad. Is everything okay?"

"Hey, Pumpkin. Everything is all right. I just wanted to go over some details about the upcoming trip."

Ever since her mother had passed away fifteen years ago, they'd spent anywhere from two weeks to a month traveling through Greece and Turkey. Mostly because Delia's father was from Greece, and he enjoyed showing her his old stomping grounds. But more than that, he enjoyed unloading all of his Greek mythology and history knowledge on her. Delia didn't mind; she enjoyed the trips and spending every ounce of time with her father that she could.

As much as she didn't feel like traveling, maybe it was what she needed mentally. A change, and a break from reality, which, in her opinion, sucked.

Withholding a sigh, she bit her bottom lip. "Mmhmmm?"

"I think we should stay for a month this time. Remember last year passed too quickly? I think it'd be good for us."

They never stayed in one place too long, which made it fun. And her father was right. Plus, it wasn't as if she had a job to anchor her anywhere.

"Yeah? You think?" Delia turned away from her computer and stood up. "A month away would be nice, but are you sure you can get away for that long?"

Her father chuckled on the other end of the phone. "Perks of being the boss, honey. I don't have to be in the office. I can work while we're on vacation."

"Doesn't that defeat the purpose?" She laughed.

"Kind of, but we both need the change of scenery, I think."

True enough. Through her many health scares, Delia had seen the toll it took on her father. It wasn't so much the physical signs, like dark circles beneath his eyes, but it was more his need to check in with her constantly via texting or phone calls. She could only assume it dredged up the horrific memories of watching his wife wither away before him. By the time Delia's mother had been diagnosed with ovarian cancer, they didn't have long with her. It was a rapid decline. As difficult as it was, she and her father still cherished their last memories with her.

"Well, as of right now, I have nothing planned. At the rate I'm going, I don't think I'll have any bites on my resume." Delia sighed. Who wanted a young woman who would have to work from home often and perhaps spend time in the hospital at random?

Likely, no one.

"Shoot. The lawyer is calling. I've got to let you go, Pumpkin. Love you, talk soon."

Once the call ended, Delia opened her e-mail app. She had two new emails from different companies regarding her resume and job opportunities. A month and a half without a job passed surprisingly quickly, but it was funny how once there was no reason to get up in the morning—or put on *real* clothes—the days blurred together.

She opened the first one and didn't read past the opening line, which was full of regret. "We regret to inform you," Delia muttered. "My ass." The next email was no better.

The most infuriating thing was that Delia loved her job. She loved working, creating graphics, and coming up with ideas for public relations. All the marketing her previous employer had done was her idea. It had been one of the most successful quarters for the construction company in a long time.

Frustrated, she took her laptop out onto the balcony of her apartment and settled in to apply for more jobs.

The view from here was her favorite. Beyond the small

park, which boasted tall palm trees, the harbor was in clear view. The sun reflected off the water, scattering across the rolling waves, lending the surface a gem-like appearance. At night, she could hear the *plupluplup* of the boat engines as they docked. But it was the sunset that took her breath away every evening with its purples, blues, and golds.

Sitting down, she focused on finishing the five new applications she'd filled out. All she could do was take a deep breath and ask whatever Fates were listening in to pull their magical strings and make sure everything was all right.

The next morning, Delia received a phone call from a potential employer. Nerves rattled her as they always did, no matter how often she endured interviews. Something about selling herself didn't settle well with her, but she'd give it her all, like she did with everything.

With a pen in hand, Delia took a deep breath and started the gut-twisting process.

The interview passed by in a blur, all warbled voices and forced laughter. By the time the painful forty minutes had passed, Delia was wrung out emotionally.

Hope could invigorate a person, but the mixed feelings of hope and doubt were exhausting.

Sloan's Ice Cream Shop called her name in the worst way.

By early noontime, the sun had heated Delia's car to the point that she could fry an egg on her black dashboard. "This is the worst year," she muttered, slipping into her leather seat. "Mother cluckin' a..." Growling in frustration, she turned the A/C on, then drove away. There was no way she was not getting Sloan's mixed berry stracciatella.

When she arrived at Rosemary Square, Delia all but raced to Sloan's. The pink doors and orange accents contrasted with the otherwise bone-white building. Before she even made it to the door, the smell of freshly cooked waffle cones and bowls tickled her senses. As much as she enjoyed the crunch of the cone, she debated on whether to go extreme. Extreme like...

A boy with short-cropped hair and a massive gap in his front teeth walked out of the shop, grinning from ear to ear as he looked down at his bucket of ice cream. Not a small, cute bucket like a toddler could carry, but a good-sized one that was overflowing with ice cream, whipped cream, and graham crackers. *That* was the extreme Delia needed... and she needed it now.

In line, she waited until it was nearly her turn, then watched as the workers slipped from behind the counter and carried a massive order of ice cream to an awaiting table. It wasn't a bowl, or even a bucket; it was practically a kitchen sink, full of a mountain of cookies, graham crackers, and, somewhere at the bottom she assumed, ice cream.

For a moment, Delia wondered if her situation was that

dire, but decided it wasn't. A bucket would do fine. Otherwise, she'd need a kitchen sink to evacuate the contents of her stomach.

One worker reappeared behind the counter. A smile tugged at her lips, and she nearly buzzed with energy. Perhaps the sugar had just leaked into her.

"What can I get you?"

Decisions, decisions. "The sandcastle sundae with the mixed berry stracciatella, and yes to everything that comes with it." After paying, Delia moved to a seat and waited for the bucket to arrive.

A well of emotions bubbled up. The longer she sat by herself, the more time she had to dwell on her current situation. All of it: the break up, the loss of her job... It felt like everything in her life was crumbling. By the time the worker brought her pail, she was almost in tears.

"Thank you," Delia murmured as she picked up her spoon. The first spoonful was heaven, but on the second, Delia almost choked on it as she cried.

If it hadn't been Delia's life, she would have thought it was a romantic comedy, and that she, the poor protagonist, was something to laugh and "aww" over. But this was real, and it plain sucked. The whole year: Jacob not believing how sick she was, the hospital, and then being fired. What more could the Fates drop at her feet?

Midway through a bite, Delia's phone rang. It was her dad again. "Mmm?" She sniffled.

"Where are you? We can meet for lunch today. I can clear all of my meetings and postpone them."

Oh, Dad... Delia's heart squeezed, knowing her father would cancel everything to whisk her away and brighten her day. "No. Don't do that. I'm eating ice cream at Sloan's..." Her voice cracked, which she had fought hard against, because Delia knew her father would only...

"Oh, Pumpkin. You're going to be all right. Take a deep breath, and know no matter what, I love you and I'm proud of you."

...do that. He would do that and open the floodgates. Tears rolled down her cheeks, splashing down onto the checkered tabletop. "I know. Thank you. I know I'm going to be okay, it's just... I really liked this job."

Her father sighed on the other end. "I know. I can help you find a similar position if you'd like. Before you say anything... I realize you don't want a position handed to you, but you always have a place here at Energesco. You're brilliant with marketing and publicizing things."

As much as Delia didn't want to admit it, she was very much a spoiled brat. Her father was an immigrant from Greece. He'd come to the states when he was only eleven years old, but he worked his tail off for everything he had today. Alexander Rentumis didn't know how to relax, not really. But he'd built his energy company from the ground up, finding fresh ways to conserve and help companies achieve green energy.

When he met Delia's mother, Tina, it was love at first sight, or so her father said. They'd given Delia a fairytale kind of life, but the happily ever after soured. Her mother died. Delia's health was now failing, and she was jobless on top of it all.

"I'll think about it. But right now, I just want to think of the beautiful beaches in Greece."

Her father laughed. "So... a month it is, then?"

"Hell yes."

Paper crinkled on the other end of the phone, and the sound of scribbling came through too. "All right. Time will fly by, and before you know it, we will be there."

"Not soon enough." Delia stared down into the dwindling amount of ice cream. How did it disappear so quickly? She frowned and eyed her phone's screen. "I'll see you soon, Dad."

She hung up and debated finishing the last quarter of the ice cream, but it sat in her belly like a brick instead of like the light, airy treat she'd wanted.

There was no need for the pail. Since she didn't want a dairy mess in her car, and there was no kid around to enjoy the bucket, Delia returned it to the counter and left the shop.

The humid air slapped her in the face again.

When Delia was little, playing with her American Girl doll, she'd always imagined that by the time she was twenty-four, she'd be married with a baby on her hip. Although by no means was she ancient, it'd always been on her list of things she wanted in life. But now? She felt as though she'd known more when she was ten than she did now.

Delia

The tinny voice of the flight attendant crackled to life at the airport's terminal. Delia's father muttered something under his breath, but Delia's eyes were trained on her phone's screen.

A reply from one of her most recent applications as a publicist for a well-to-do law firm popped up. She exhaled shakily. It'd been two entire months since they had fired her, and she really, *really* wanted a new job to fill her empty days.

"Delia, we're next," her father prompted, tugging on the end of her braid.

Delia's eyes dragged up from her screen, and she stood up automatically. She tugged along her luggage as she finally opened the email.

We regret to inform you...

Delia locked her phone and shook her head. "What is wrong with me?" It was a rhetorical question, but her father wasn't going to let that one go.

"Nothing. Anyone would be lucky to have you as an employee."

Delia didn't need to look over her shoulder to know her father was beaming at her, his gaze full of pride and the typical crooked smile on his lips. She rolled her eyes, wondering why, if that was true, was she jobless still? He was always so sure of her, but why didn't she feel the same way?

With a sigh, she twisted to look at him. There it was, just as she expected. The look of a proud, beaming father.

"What would make you happy, kamari mou?"

His pride. Oh, to have it be founded.

Delia handed over her ticket and identification, musing over the question. "I mean, I'm not *not* happy. I've just had a rough few months... and it's hard coming up for air when more crap is just hurled on top." She visualized drowning in the middle of the Atlantic, pawing at the water for purchase, only for a giant wave to crash down on her, pushing her deeper into the bottomless sea.

They moved onto the plane and found their seats.

Delia's father pressed his lips together, brows pinching like they usually did when he was in deep thought. "Whatever it is in life that will give you joy, that's what I wish for you. Whether it's a dream job, a wonderful partner, or sitting with your old man on Psarou Beach."

Shoving her carry-on into the compartment above, she laughed. "I'll take the last over everything else. What better way to spend my days than with my ass in the sand with my dad?"

Her father chuckled and settled against the seat. His tan hand patted Delia's knee. "You know the way to my heart."

Delia smiled and put her earbuds in, settling in for a long flight from Miami to Istanbul. In around twelve hours' time, she'd be in one of her favorite places, and reality would seem like a distant dream.

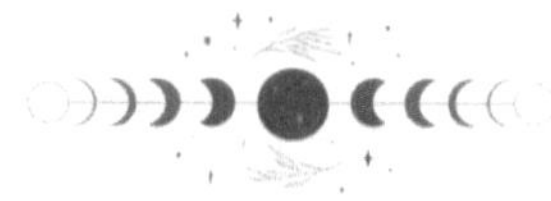

Apparently, Delia had needed sleep. She didn't wake until the tires hit the tarmac, and the pilot's heavy use of the brake jarred her against the plane's window. She frowned as the soft tendrils of a deep and wonderful sleep left her.

Where was she?

She wiped the sleep from her eyes, faintly recalling the dream she'd left behind. A tanned man's torso bare before her. The glint of intelligent and playful hazel eyes. The flash of a golden arrow.

"One thing I neglected to tell you before you started snoring is that we're staying at the Çırağan Palace. There were no rooms available at our usual spot. I guess they're renovating, which decreases their capacity." He shrugged. "I hope we'll make fresh memories at Çırağan."

Delia laughed. The way her father spoke about Çırağan, it was as if it were subpar, but it was one of the most eye-pleasing buildings she'd ever seen. On the shore of the Bosporus, it boasted a grand view of the water. But it wasn't just that; it had once been an Ottoman Palace, and still looked very much like one. Outside, several pillars appeared to hold the weathered ivory stone up, and while the carved stone with its embellished accents were lovely, the inside was breathtaking.

"Dad, I'm going to love the Çırağan. I've wanted to stay there before." When it was their turn, she stood up and grabbed her carry-on. "I'm actually really looking forward to this." The inside of that hotel was enough to squeal over. Marble floors, walls, and bathrooms. Chandeliers and spiral staircases. Beautiful artwork on the ceilings... She'd be staying in a palace instead of a cold, contemporary luxury hotel.

Her father's expression softened as he bent to kiss her head. "I'm glad. We'll have to leave earlier, since we won't be as close to Selçuk as usual."

Selçuk was a five-hour trip in a rental car, or double that via bus. Delia wanted no part of a ten-hour bus trip after traveling for half a day in a plane.

Once they disembarked, the smells of the airport taunted her. Spiced meats, buttery pastries... *Food.* She desperately needed food, and the restaurants down the corridor called to Delia like a siren's lethal song. At least eating wouldn't be her demise. Hopefully.

"Let's grab something to eat since I screwed myself by sleeping on the plane." It was already five o'clock in the evening, which meant she *should* be winding down shortly, but after sleeping for twelve hours, all she wanted to do was buzz around.

Her father nodded. "It's a date... after our luggage arrives."

Delia whined. "There are *plenty* of places in Greece that wouldn't mind our lack of clothing. Or in the very least, my lack of clothing."

"I wouldn't appreciate it. At all. Besides, we're in Istanbul." Her father's bushy brows slanted inward, the stern expression marring his handsome face.

"Well, luckily, my body isn't meant for you, it's meant for someone else. And we'll be heading to Greece after Turkey. Still time to hit those nude beaches." She winked at him, laughing as he grunted.

On arrival at Çırağan Palace, Delia slid from the cab and froze. Before her, gold light illuminated the structure, giving the building a heavenly glow. Shadows created by the light added depth to the pillars and carved stone. It didn't matter how many pictures Delia took; they could never do the building justice.

Despite that, she took out her phone and snapped several pictures of the landscaping, the beautifully lit pillars, the Bosphorus Strait.

Honestly, she'd seen nothing so beautiful in her life.

"Come here." She motioned to her father and leaned in close to him, capturing a selfie in front of the building.

He brushed a kiss to her temple, then moved to gather their luggage from the trunk.

Unlike Delia, her father had bags under his eyes, and the weight of jet lag settled on his shoulders heavily; she could tell he was exhausted. She grabbed her suitcase from him, and together they made it inside.

"Dad, you should head to the room. I'm not going to be sleeping any time soon." He shot her a dubious look. "I'll be fine." Motioning to the breathtaking view of the marble interior, she laughed. "Do you see this? I can't possibly go to our room before taking at least a fraction of this in."

"All right. Leave your suitcase here, and your carry-on. I'll get a key for you."

He ventured to the desk to speak to guest services. Meanwhile, Delia spun around, glancing up at the ceiling. Golds, soft browns, and ivory came to life beneath the candlelit bulbs.

She'd spent a good portion of her time overseas in luxurious hotels, but this one by far took the cake.

What would it have been like to live in this place when it was a palace? Oh, she knew. Delia knew all the history surrounding Turkey and Greece, having grown up listening to it and reading about it. But to truly live in such a time when the gods—whether or not they were real—supposedly walked among them in disguise; wouldn't that have been something?

Despite everything that had happened lately, happiness swelled within. The sound of a piano's notes echoed off the marble walls and flooring. It took Delia a moment to realize it was "Perfect" by Ed Sheeran.

Ugh, this song. It was so perfect, as was this place.

A tap on the shoulder brought her back to reality, and Delia twirled to face her father. "Have you seen this place?" She gaped in awe at the complete craftsmanship of the inside.

Her father chuckled. "I know, but wait until you see the view from our room. On one of my trips with your mother, we stayed in the same room I booked for us. Ah, she loved it. I haven't been here since." He frowned, making it clear he was thinking of his wife and the time they shared in the hotel. "When they said the rooms were all booked up in Izmir, this was the second place I thought of. So many memories... I thought you'd enjoy spending time in a place your mother loved so much." His eyes glazed over as, Delia assumed, he took a trip down memory lane. "Anyway, here is your room key. We're in the Pasha Presidential Suite. Don't stay up too late, or you'll really screw with your sleep schedule." He winked, then turned down to the elevators, disappearing moments later.

Drawn back outside, Delia walked along the concrete path. Winding around the garden to the pool, then toward the sunbathing deck. She pressed herself against the stone railing and marveled at how close she was to the Bosphorus. Waves lapped against the stone wall as a ferry hummed along the strait, but the sound of a man on the loudspeaker ruined the otherwise peaceful setting. Still, Delia couldn't believe it was right there. More than that, the glow from the hotel cast a warmth into the sky and onto the strait, turning it a deep, gem-like blue.

Tomorrow would begin the road to recovery. An entire month to heal the wounds of her breakup and the loss of her job. All she needed was rest, relaxation, and a little distraction. As far as distractions went, Delia thought this was a good place to start. With so much beauty surrounding her, how could she be miserable?

No, she wouldn't invite that question to linger, because she knew the answer. *Easily, easily.* Anything could turn to ash in an instant.

"Enjoy your time, Delia," she murmured to herself. "There is a season for everything, right? Well, I'm deciding it's the season of healing." A breeze spun off the water, pimpling her skin with goosebumps. "And also time to go back inside."

A little more exploring, a little more walking around, and then maybe it would be time to settle down with a book.

THREE

Delia

The next morning, the bright tendrils of the sun awakened Delia. She'd forgotten to close the drapes, and her bed faced the rising sun. Groaning, she slid from bed and explored the suite, made herself a cup of coffee, then ventured out onto her room's balcony.

"Ah! You were right." Delia took a breath of the fresh air. She flicked her dark gaze over to her father, drinking tea on his own balcony, and grinned.

"Did you even look at the suite?" He shook his head, chuckling.

Delia ducked back inside the room and walked around to her father's balcony. "I did! Now I'm tempted to leap into the water. I'm part mermaid after all."

He turned his head as she entered. Something flickered in her father's eyes, as if he were reliving a memory again, then he shook his head. "No. Not a mermaid. I think you once declared yourself 'Helen of West Palm Beach.'"

"I thought it was a pretty name, and the idea of Helen of

Troy fascinated me when I was little. Not now. Besides, I prefer to think of myself as a mermaid. If Ariel can get legs, I can get fins, right?" She wrinkled her nose up, laughing. "You don't know what's in store for me."

"And if I did, perhaps I wouldn't tell you. It's never wise to know about your future."

What would happen if one knew too much about their future? Would that alter it? If her father had known how little time he'd have with his wife, would he have chosen a different life partner? Would Delia exist? It was a labyrinth of questions, and she supposed each decision led a person down a different line of fate.

Delia popped her lips together. "Fine. We have to be out the door in five minutes. Our rental car was delivered a half hour ago according to the alert on my phone, and we've got at least a five-hour drive ahead of us. Our tour starts at one, so we should have more than enough time."

Peering over his mug, her father inclined his head. "I'll be ready, don't you worry."

In five minutes, as promised, her father was ready. Dressed in his casual khakis and polo shirt, he looked comfortable. Sometimes Delia forgot what he looked like outside of his business suits.

Since Delia had learned her lesson a few years ago, she wore a pair of sneakers instead of flats. It was all about being casual with the amount of walking they were going to do. She wore a white button-up blouse and a pair of navy-striped high-waisted shorts.

The sun felt like a warm blanket against her skin. She'd

take that over Florida's humid heat any day. At least she could breathe without feeling as if she were suffocating. Putting her sunglasses on her head, Delia flicked her braid over her shoulder and motioned for her father to lead the way out of the room.

Downstairs and outside of the lobby, the car waited in the valet area.

Clucking her tongue, Delia ticked things off on her fingers. "Purse, phone, wallet... Am I missing anything?" She glanced up, looking around. "Dad? I'm missing Dad." Her brows pinched together as she scanned the immediate area, only to find him at the gateway to the property.

He waved from a distance and jogged toward the car. "Sorry. Just taking pictures."

"I could've left without you." She grinned, slipping into the silver SUV's driver seat. "Get some tunes on, we're kicking off this trip with a soundtrack." Slipping her sunglasses down, she pulled out of the parking lot and settled in. Surprisingly—or not so surprisingly—her father picked a pop station. The tune was catchy, but the singer's high-pitched tone grated on her nerves. He was no Usher.

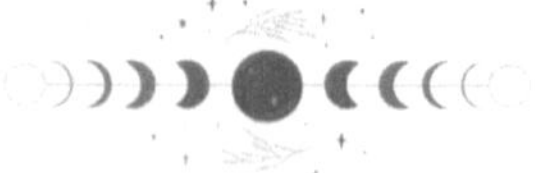

After several traffic jams and necessary pit stops, they arrived at the Selçuk Museum where the tour bus waited... or should have been waiting.

"Shit! No, no, no..." She turned the SUV off and scrambled for her belongings. Her father snored in his seat, drooling onto his lap. It was likely the only reason she'd gotten away with swearing, but it wouldn't surprise her if he woke up now and chastised her for it.

"Dad, we're here, and we have to hurry."

He slurped the drool up with a snort, which resulted in a hacking cough. "I'm all right, I'm all right."

Heart pounding in her chest, Delia bolted from the vehicle. "I'm going to see if we can grab another bus." *Good thing I remembered my running shoes.* As she ran inside the air-conditioned building, she collided with a body with enough force that they both rocked back. But strong hands held Delia in place, then steadied both of them.

"Whoa." A pair of luminous hazel eyes blinked down at her, squinting with barely restrained laughter. He said something in what was probably Turkish, because definitely it wasn't Greek; Delia would've understood him if it was.

Pushing the sunglasses up, she took a moment too long to drink in his features. Dark olive skin and inky black hair that contrasted with those ridiculously beautiful eyes. Lashes that long had no business on a man, especially this man. Color rushed into her tan cheeks, and she at least had the decency to look abashed.

She tried speaking in English. Most of the museum workers spoke it well, considering it was one of the highlighted tourist spots. Delia pegged him for an employee due to the name tag on his sports jacket that read *Conner*. "I'm sorry. We missed the tour bus." She groaned. "It's important. I go on this trip every year with my dad, and it's really cheesy, maybe, but I look forward to it."

He lifted his brows in surprise, then his lips pressed together. Was he annoyed, or getting ready to tell her to get lost? But then a smile broke out on his face, and he held up a finger. The young man jogged to the counter and leaned over, tugging out a keychain. He said something to another museum employee, then returned to Delia.

"I have a solution for you: your own tour guide. Where's your ticket?" He nodded to her hands.

"Oh! Yes." Delia pulled her phone out and opened the email with their tickets. "Here." She glanced up at him, daring another look as he peered down.

He plucked his phone from his pocket and scanned the QR code. "Very nice, Delia, is it? Now I don't have to escort you from the premises." It was difficult to discern if he was joking or not, but it didn't matter because in the next moment, his head dipped. "My name is Conner Velis," he said with a voice as smooth and sweet as honey, then he swept into a bow. "Your chariot awaits you. Or, at the very least, a moderately clean sedan with air conditioning."

Delia laughed. "Hey, that's more than some can say..." Conner's gaze focused over her shoulder, forcing Delia to spin around to face her dad as he walked into the museum. "Okay, so we totally missed the bus, but Conner is going to drive us." She lifted her eyebrows as she stared at her father, willing him to tear his eyes away from Conner. But he didn't.

Her father's face shifted from surprised to dubious. "Can I see a form of identification?"

Conner chuckled, pulling his lanyard up from under his shirt. "Good thinking, Dad. I'm one of the tour guides here at the Ephesus Archaeological Museum. I should be on lunch, but I can make an exception for a private tour. Since I don't want to be the one responsible for breaking tradition."

Delia tugged on the back of her father's shirt as he leaned in to inspect the ID. "Okay. Are you going to ask for the manager too?"

"Unfortunately, you can't be too careful." Her father frowned at her and stepped back.

"I agree, but a private tour sounds wonderful." Plus, in Delia's opinion, the guy was gorgeous. "Thank you, Conner, that sounds perfect."

Conner slid his phone into his back pocket and fiddled with his keys as he waited for them to decide whether or not they'd take him up on his offer.

Delia peered over her shoulder. "Just a second, Conner." She opened the door and motioned for her father to step outside. Why did her father look so perturbed? It wasn't her fault they'd missed the bus, and she even landed a private tour.

"Remember, I'm here to forget the shitty—" Delia bit the tip of her tongue, scrunching her nose at her father's silent reprimand. "Crappy few months. Look how gorgeous he is. I know better than to be an idiot. The curse of being a female:

you always have to be aware of your surroundings and who you're dealing with." She thought she had been speaking quietly, but the clearing of a throat behind her said otherwise.

Her father's eyebrows lifted in mild amusement, but it also looked like another reprimand was on the way. Wincing, he motioned toward the museum.

Delia cringed. "Is he behind me?"

Conner chuckled. "I am, but I'm used to tuning out TMI from tourists." He glanced at the sidewalk, as if it were about to open up and devour him. "Anyway... this is a company car. It has a GPS system that my boss can tap into if I go on a joy ride during working hours. She can override the system and shut it down. Which, I'll have you know, she has not had to do in... many years." He motioned to the car as he approached it and unlocked it. "Hop in and we'll get started."

Delia went to slide into the front seat, but her father took it instead. She *harrumphed* and slid into the seat behind Conner. Her eyes met his in the rearview mirror, and she couldn't help but smile. Something about the energy surrounding him, swirling in his gaze, elicited excitement.

Conner and her father started talking as the car purred to life, but Delia checked out for a moment, reassuring herself that she could have fun. She wanted to forget home, its circumstances, and what wasn't waiting for her there. Delia wanted to heal, relax, even live a little. What was wrong with a little harmless flirting while she was on vacation?

Year after year, she reminded herself, she'd been forced to grow up quickly when her mother became sick. And when her own health rapidly declined, the panic and anxiety that had filled her was horrible.

"So, you said it was tradition to come here. How many times have you been? Do I need to skip my touristy speech?" Conner laughed, abruptly tearing Delia from her thoughts.

"Fifteen times," she replied, squinting her eyes as she counted on her fingers. "This year marks fifteen."

The car turned down a familiar road, leading them away from the heavily populated area and down a dirt country road.

"No need to bore you with the history of the grounds and temple, then. You know everything about it."

Delia knew almost everything about it, unless he had new information that had been added to their literature recently. But she wanted to hear him talk. How he enunciated things, and the way it sounded like he was smiling with every word.

Quiet filled the car, then Conner tapped his window with his knuckles. "I've got it. Did you know that Artemis had a favorite hound? His name was Kítrinos. A mortal wounded him gravely when they were at war with Olympus. She never got over him, but that mortal was turned into a squealing boar and wound up on the table of his own men's feast. A fitting ending for his life, no?" Conner glanced into the mirror, lifting his dark eyebrows in question.

So, he was a storyteller? She supposed it came with the job.

"That is interesting..." Delia peered into the front seat, took one look at her father's face, and started laughing silently. Her shoulders shook, but no sound escaped. He looked both disturbed and surprised at the quick conjuring of the tale.

The car wound down a dirt road, giving way to a small grassy knoll. In the distance, columns jutted from the earth. Artemis' temple ruins. Turning the car off, Conner opened the door and leaned against the roof, admiring the view.

"And here we are. What remains of the once beautiful temple."

Acontius

Acontius' heart pounded wildly in his chest. The name he'd taken in the mortal realm was Conner Velis, since Acontius wasn't a name that rolled off the tongue easily, nor was it a modern name.

A lie to mask his truth.

Somehow, he'd kept his act together at the museum when Delia ran into him. It had been an entire year since he'd last seen her and, on a foolish whim, bound her to him with an apple. Every day since then, he'd been kicking himself because it was only a matter of time before Artemis found out, and the repercussions of his idiocy would be severe.

But as Acontius watched Delia stare over the ruins, Artemis' wrath felt like a distant thing. Her dark, luminous eyes flicked toward him, and he felt his heart stutter. She was *beautiful*. Chestnut hair, sun-kissed skin, bottomless brown eyes. And now that he'd spoken to her and experienced a fraction of her personality, Acontius was certain he'd made the right decision.

A decision so asinine that he'd assumed Eros had crossed Artemis by targeting him. But none were so stupid as to bother the Goddess of the Hunt's pack.

The buzzing of his mobile phone pulled Acontius from his thoughts, and when he glanced down at the screen, he blanched.

Artemis.

He couldn't ignore the call. If she'd dialed in to his GPS, she'd see where he was...

Answering the phone, he turned his back on Delia and her father. "Hello, Arty."

On the other end, Artemis sighed. "Where are you?"

"A late tour group showed up at the museum. They had tickets already, and I didn't want them to miss out."

"I didn't realize we gave private tours now. Never mind. When you're done with them, come and find me. It's about my brother."

A pit formed in Acontius' stomach. What was Apollo up to? He frowned at the phone as the call ended.

It'd been one hundred years since Apollo's wrath had fallen on the land in the form of a pandemic. Was he about to unleash another punishment for gods only knew what reason?

"Hey." Delia appeared by his side, head cocked in curiosity. "Are you okay? You look like someone just ran over your dog."

Acontius grinned at her, laughing. "No, it was the boss. I

told you she'd home in on me. Anyway, why don't we walk around the temple? I'll spare you the usual speech and story-telling." He drew a cross over his heart. "Promise."

"I'm ready when you are." Delia peered over her shoulder at her father and then back to Acontius. "And you can tell us wild stories of Artemis in her glory days, if you'd like."

He lifted his dark brows, lips twisting in thought. "Really? Well, I'm sure I can think of a few stories..." Walking around the car, he took the lead and followed the dirt path down to the ruins on the grass. There was a small, beat-up pillar with more rubble next to it. This was where Acontius had first seen Delia, where he'd thrown the apple at her feet and bound them together.

A warm breeze caressed his face, cooling his heated skin. The sun was high in the noon sky, and thankfully, Acontius had forgotten his sports jacket in the museum's break room. Sighing, he rolled his sleeves up to his elbows and turned on his heel, only to find Delia staring at him.

"Sorry. I was just wondering... Why do you think they never rebuilt the temple again? I mean, I know it kept being ruined, but if Artemis had such a large following..."

Acontius smiled as Delia's curiosity ran wild, and luck-ily, he knew the answer well. "I suspect it's largely because of the leaders' fickle minds and what they believed was right. When Olympus fell, so did the gods. Humankind didn't believe in them anymore, so what was the point in building temples for fellowship if they found new gods to worship? While Artemis had a great following, they fell victim to new laws, new ways to praise..." Acontius' words trailed as he surveyed the land, but when he turned back and saw Delia's gaze zoned in on him with an intensity he hadn't seen earlier, his stomach fluttered.

A throat cleared, disrupting the moment. "Can we continue?" Delia's father looked semi-peeved.

"Of course." In a few strides, Acontius took the lead again, winding their way through the ruins, down to the still-standing structure.

Chipped columns stretched toward the sky, stubbornly holding on to their purchase, even though the surrounding walls had crumbled to dust long ago. Stone stairs, although broken in some areas, still remained in place.

Memories flooded Acontius. He remembered the first time he'd entered the temple, ushered in by Artemis. His aunt, forced to keep her distance from him, smiling at him. The vow he took to remain pure to Artemis' Order. The irony of breaking the vow on sacred grounds wasn't lost on him. Although, he hadn't truly broken a vow. He was still pure—save for tossing an apple at Delia's feet, he hadn't acted on any impulse.

Yet.

As the sun faded into the sky, his voice grew hoarse from the amount of talking he'd done. And eventually, it was time to leave the premises.

"Where do you stay when you aren't working?" Delia broke through the silence that had settled between them.

Rubbing the back of his neck, he chuckled. "An apartment close to the museum."

"Oh." She looked thoughtful, and then, "When is your next day off?"

What a bold question. Acontius leaned against the car's hood and stroked his chin playfully. "Why? Already missing my wealth of information?"

Delia's cheeks reddened. She toyed with the end of the braid on her shoulder, fidgeting. "I thought we could meet up and talk about your absurd amount of knowledge about Artemis." She lowered her voice, leaning in toward him. "I'm in Istanbul at the Çırağan."

"Oh, you're staying at a palace! And you're consorting with the likes of a mere poor boy."

Delia snorted. "Give me a break. If you're interested in talking more, I'll be here for another two weeks. Do you want my number?"

What was he supposed to say? His mouth hung open in surprise, but his hand extended his mobile device. "Uh, yeah. Sure." She typed her number in and labeled her contact name as "Delia" with a bow and arrow emoji. *Artemis. Hunter.*

She had no idea how close she was to the mark.

When Acontius slid into the driver's seat, he felt a hard gaze piercing the side of his face. Reluctantly, he met the intense, dark eyes of Delia's father, who he knew as Alexander Rentumis. Last year, after his thoughtless action of rolling the apple toward Delia, he'd made it a point to interact with who he had rightfully assumed to be her father. He'd learned far more about the man in a five-minute conversation in an open field than Acontius had ever expected to. Alexander was a good man, a good father. And judging by the way Alexander was staring at him, he remembered Acontius' face and was likely trying to figure out how and why.

After closing the museum, Acontius thought he'd avoided Artemis. She'd vanished into the back, and he assumed she'd stepped through a portal. But as he locked down the last part of the museum, the sound of footsteps echoed in the silent building.

"Acontius." Artemis spoke his name with a commanding edge to it. "We have a budding problem."

His stomach dropped. Panic crept up his neck and rushed into his cheeks, coloring them. "What?"

"Apollo has tired of the mortals and their lack of respect for... much of anything." Artemis scoffed, flipping her hand as she walked across the room to close the distance between them. She was tall without heels, and when she wore them as she did now, Artemis stood two inches above his six feet. By no means was she a delicate looking woman. Although slender, she was built like an athlete, and her shrewd hazel eyes could pierce anyone's soul.

"Without Olympus, there is very little power to draw on. What is the point of his tantrum?"

Artemis clicked her tongue, wagging a finger at him. "Watch your mouth." She sighed, flicking a strand of raven-black hair out of her face. "He thinks he can restore Olympus, and maybe we could if we band together, but he wants to cleanse the world first."

None of this information soothed Acontius' worries; it only confirmed them. Apollo was going to try to unleash a plague... again. His modern plagues were not like his biblical plagues of old on a smaller scale. The 1918 Spanish Flu: his doing. Swine Flu, Bird Flu: his attempts at conjuring a plague of old. But without the ability to draw on power, he couldn't level the earth like he once had.

"No," Acontius breathed. "He can't do that." What of Delia? Her father? What of the vow ...

"No, he can't. I agree. Very seldom do I step in, but I cannot stand behind this. When it comes time, we'll need a distraction." Artemis' eyes assessed him, and she tapped a finger to her lips. "Be ready. That is all I ask."

"As you wish, my lady." He bowed to her and felt her hand rest against the nape of his neck.

"I'll lock up. Sleep well, hunter."

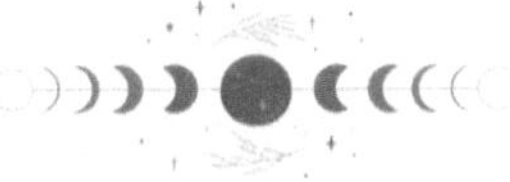

Over the next three days, Acontius hardly slept, and his mind raced with the possibilities of what would soon unfold.

Another battle, another war... and this time against the highly protective brother of Artemis, Apollo.

Stress oozed into every pore of Acontius. Of course, it didn't help he was waiting to see if Delia would text him first—she didn't.

He was the one who broke down and texted her, which was why he was driving to Istanbul despite living in Selçuk. Fortunately, it was early morning, which meant he could spend most of the day with Delia. And, worst-case scenario, he'd spend the night at a local hotel and leave in the early morning. The Çırağan was a little out of his budget.

Upon arrival, Acontius stared at the gateway to the parking lot. The hotel reminded him of Artemis' temple in its prime: beautiful, breathtaking, awe-inspiring, and humbling.

After finding a parking spot, he pulled his mobile out and texted Delia, but a tap on his shoulder had him spinning around. "Oh, hey." Delia stood in front of him, eyes glittering in excitement as she looked up at him.

"Well, good morning, Conner. I wasn't sure what to expect, but I like this." She motioned to his wardrobe, which wasn't anything to write home about: a pair of khaki shorts, a teal button-up shirt, and instead of smoothed back hair, he'd allowed his natural waves their freedom.

One brow arched. "Should I have worn my uniform?"

Delia stammered. "No, I mean... you look amazing. Fine, I mean." She flushed, looking down at her white shoes.

"Hey, don't be like that. I'm teasing." Acontius reached for her, his fingers lightly grazing her chin to turn it up. "I don't know about you, but I need breakfast before I do anything else." He flexed his fingers as he drew his hand away. The touch sent an electric pulse through him.

Delia didn't flinch away, but she gaped at him. She lifted her hand and brushed where he'd touched. "The restaurant inside is good. Let's grab something there."

Acontius nodded, motioning for her to lead the way.

After a filling breakfast and light-hearted conversations, the tone took a darker turn when Delia started to discuss her recent mishaps. The breakup. Her health. It was a quick change to her demeanor. Her expression shifted; clouds rolled across her bright face.

All Acontius could do was listen. He had no sage advice to offer. He didn't want to press his luck anyway because, well, who was he? A strange guy she'd met at a museum.

Frowning, Delia poked at a berry on her plate. "I'm going to be honest with you, and I don't know why. I'm a wreck. I don't know when I'm going to be pieced together again. I've had two relationships end in one year. The first one was because he couldn't handle my health issues, the second one claimed I was faking my poor health."

"What do you mean about your health? Are you sick?" Acontius leaned forward, placing his elbows on the table, unsure of how much she'd continue to talk about her personal life. But he'd take everything she gave to him.

She sighed. "Yes... No. No one knows what's wrong, but every time I think a relationship is 'the one,' it tanks along with my health." Throwing her hands up, Delia rested against her chair. "I don't know what's wrong."

Was this a repercussion from the vow? Acontius paled.

Delia clammed up as the server returned with their check. She paid for it quickly and collected her purse. "Anyway, I didn't mean to put a damper on our morning."

"You didn't. I feel like I should offer something of myself now." His lips twisted as he sat back, fingers drumming on the table. "I'm not sure what. I'm actually rather boring." In this lifetime, he was. Separated from the world of the gods, forced to live a mortal's life in an immortal body.

Delia's eyes sparked with life again, and a slow smile spread across her face. "Why do I doubt that?"

Acontius' eyes flicked to the table, then back up at her. "I don't know." He smiled crookedly and sprung to his feet. "You'll have to tell me after today." Extending his hand to her, he waited until she stood, then tugged on her hand to reel her closer. She stood inches from him. Close enough that he could smell the floral shampoo she used.

"What?" Delia laughed as he tugged her along the pathway.

Outside of the hotel, the sun caught his eyes, momentarily disorienting him as he stepped down a stair. Such a simple thing had his mind racing back to Artemis, and what they feared from Apollo. Had the sun god finally lost his patience with the modern world?

Running a hand through his hair, Acontius cleared his thoughts. Delia watched him thoughtfully, as if she were waiting. Waiting for what?

He mustered his courage, then blurted, "Let's go to Burc Beach."

"That's a bit of a drive…" Delia mused. "It's early enough that we can still get a good spot."

Acontius nodded. "It is, and that was my thought. So how about it?"

"Let's do it."

Grabbing Delia's hand, Acontius tugged her along the concrete path to the parking lot. "Then let's get our day started!" He laughed, having the decency to look bashful when a passing gentleman walked by.

FIVE

Delia

There was something so... so naïve and innocent about Conner. The glint in his eyes, though playful, wasn't full of wickedness. Delia had seen her fair share of devious glances from others and knew one when she saw one. More than that, he was so *nice*. Or at the very least, seemed nice. She was judging by what he'd shown her in a day in Selçuk and now at breakfast.

Delia knew she was getting ahead of herself, but it just felt good to have something fun. A fling, maybe? But whenever she glanced his way, there was a lack of hunger in his eyes. A part of her was disappointed because she found herself longing for something easy, simple, with no strings attached. Nothing permanent.

After they'd reached the parking lot, Delia suggested she drive, since Conner spent all morning traveling. It turned out he had far better taste in music than her father did.

Moments away from the beach, Jason Derulo came on the radio, and Acontius turned the volume up. What she expected was the sound of a goat screaming; what she heard, as Acontius opened his mouth to sing, was the same honey voice as Jason himself. *Great gods.* This guy could sing. He sounded *better* than Jason.

"Okay... you have *that* voice, but you work at a museum. Why?" Delia gaped at him as they pulled into the parking lot.

Conner turned the volume down and shrugged. "I've known my boss for a long time. Arty is like family to me. I've known her since I was born, and when she gave me the opportunity to work for her... I took it. Besides, I know more than a person should about ancient history and civilization."

It dawned on Delia then: she hadn't asked if he was single or not. "And you don't have a girlfriend?"

"No," he answered quickly. "I'd use the work excuse, but I guess when it comes down to it, I'm just a little out of my element."

How? This man was gorgeous. She didn't want to laugh at him, but it was difficult to wrap her head around it. He had to be lying—or gay, which was fine, but *she* would be lying if said that wouldn't be disappointing.

She wanted to ask how, but Conner looked as if he longed to crawl under a rock and hide until the conversation passed, so she let it go.

Delia opened the door and waited for him to exit the SUV before locking it. "Do you come up here often, or do you stay down south?"

Rounding the vehicle, he stood beside her and glanced

up from beneath his lashes. "I stay down south mostly, but I travel to Greece a lot. Most of my family is from Kea Island."

"When was the last time you saw them?"

Conner paused, twisting his lips. "A year ago. Although, I have a feeling I'll be seeing them really soon."

"I hope so. Family is important." A pang of guilt clenched her heart. She'd ditched her father to spend time with a guy she barely knew. However, aside from lecturing her about safety, he'd seemed fine with it. "After we're done in Turkey, we're off to Athens."

In front of the car, a pair of concrete stairs led the way to the beach. Delia descended and gazed out over the sand. It was filling up already, even at only ten o'clock in the morning, but it was one of the better beaches that wasn't private.

She closed her eyes, absorbing the smell of the ocean, the feel of the sun, and the knowledge that Conner was with her. When she went home to her *nothing*, she'd want to remember this blip in time.

"Are you all right?" Conner asked, moving to stand in front of her.

"I'm fine—no—I'm perfect." As she looked up at him, her stomach fluttered. His light hazel eyes were still full of concern. "Today is all about fun. So let's get to it." Delia reached her hand out for his and squeezed it before tugging him through the sand at a jog.

She laughed, truly laughed, like she hadn't in so long. She felt like a girl—like the bubbly teen that she once had been—carefree and wild. Like before her mother was sick, when she could simply focus on being a playful teen. When she could spend time with her school friends, go to the mall, and just be ridiculous.

Conner's dark hair fell into his eyes as a breeze kicked up. It only added to his boyish innocence. Where had he been hiding from life, to have not become jaded?

One moment, Delia was walking backward; the next, she was tumbling toward the ground as her foot sank into a hole.

Conner's arms slid around her middle, suspending her mid-fall. He pulled her upright, which positioned her against his chest. This was the second time he'd saved her from colliding with the ground.

Butterflies flapped their delicate wings in her belly, and a rush of warmth colored her cheeks. "I'm actually not a clumsy person," she offered quietly.

Conner's lips spread into a warm grin. "Really? You could have fooled me." He lifted his hand, brushing loose strands of her hair out of her face.

A strong urge to kiss him filled Delia. She didn't really know this guy, but the whole point of this vacation had been to live and forget the troubles at home. Thinking was the last thing she wanted to do.

This close to Conner, she didn't have much distance to close between them. He also didn't pull away the closer she drew. And when their lips met, something in her sighed. His arm drew her closer so their chests were flush against each other. Why she thought he'd stiffen and pull away was beyond her, but gods... his lips tasted like peppermint, and they felt silky smooth as they collided with hers.

Tentatively, she dragged her tongue along his, and Conner sucked in a breath, groaning at her boldness. She shivered despite the warmth of the air against them as his hands slid down to her hips, pulling hers into his.

She felt as he hardened against her lower abdomen, only intoxicating her further. Conner must have tasted the desperation on her lips, on her tongue, because he lifted his hands and cupped her face, and the kiss became frenzied, desperate.

They were still out in the open, amongst the beachgoers. None had set up their towels near them yet, but Delia wanted more of Conner. More of his body, his skin. She dragged her nails up his back, then into the soft, dark waves at the nape of his neck.

"Delia," he murmured against her lips. Pulling away, he left a fiery trail of kisses down the column of her throat. "There is nowhere to go." His light eyes opened, taking in the long, stretching beach.

He was right. No caves, no rocks to obscure the view. Just sun-bleached sand and the cold water lapping at the shore. Too cold for them, wasn't it?

Clarity entered Conner's gaze. When he pulled back, his lips were kiss-swollen and red. "Not here, not like this. You deserve more than the discomfort of sand..." His words trailed, replaced by a husky chuckle.

Still, she wanted that. But she wanted to take her time, committing every dimple, angle, and noise Conner made to memory. A gem taken from this vacation to recall on dreary days back at home.

"We're at the beach," Conner mused out loud, withdrawing. "We may as well get some swimming in, no?" Unbuttoning his shirt, he discarded it on the sand.

Without his shirt, Conner's torso was on full display. She'd felt the muscles against him but seeing them was different. Lean, cut, tan muscle flexed as he leaned away.

Delia removed her shoes, toeing them toward his shirt. She shook her head, grinning like a fool. She hadn't brought a bathing suit, which meant it would be a very damp ride back home.

"Let's go, I guess!" Delia ran toward the water, leaping over the waves and diving beneath the surface. Instead of the cold water she'd expected, it was warm. Not as warm as she was used to, but also not frigid. As she surfaced, she looked around for Conner. He was nowhere to be found. She twirled around and felt bubbles brush against her legs. Moments later, Conner surfaced behind her, arms around her midsection.

If this was just the start to her vacation, she would take it a thousand times over again.

The day was full of stolen kisses, bold caresses, and carefree fun. Delia couldn't remember the last time she'd truly enjoyed herself.

They spent time in the water, then patrolled the beachside snack shops, eating and drinking until they couldn't any longer.

Inevitably, the day turned into early evening, and it was time to return to the hotel.

Acontius

Despite not having swimming trunks, Acontius was fairly dry thanks to the hours spent talking and eating beyond the beach. He was stuffed, sunburnt, and "happy" didn't quite describe how he felt. His one regret was that the night must end.

He sat in the passenger seat of Delia's SUV, not wanting to watch her walk away. Not wanting the night—or the feeling—to end. But what were the terms of the vow? Did they mean Delia was bound to him for eternity, or for a mortal's lifetime?

Delia turned the car off. She didn't turn to look at him, which was a punch to his gut. "I don't want to go in."

Acontius smiled. He didn't either. "Well, this isn't our goodbye, not yet. It's just a goodnight." Leaning across the center console, he pressed a kiss to the corner of her mouth, and then found her lips against his in a slow, mind-numbing kiss.

Kissing. Something he'd never done before. At eight

years old, when Acontius had taken his vow, it wasn't as if he'd had an opportunity to kiss girls. The women around him were of Artemis' Order, and it was forbidden to touch them, or else she'd turn him into a hound—or worse.

But it was no wonder the other gods spent so much time fooling around if a kiss was only a fraction of what sex could elicit from him. Gods. Delia's mouth was sweeter than any honey mead he'd ever tasted, and the feeling that sparked deep inside him was a primal urge.

This was what he'd sworn to never partake in. This was breaking a vow. But Acontius wanted more. He wanted it never to end.

Sighing, he withdrew. "Good night, Delia." He opened the car door and stepped out, waiting for her to do the same. His arms encircled her as she sprung at him, and their lips sought one another's out again, drawing out the inevitable departure.

"Good night," Delia echoed, pulling away. Halfway toward the entrance, she spun around to wave at him, then disappeared into the hotel.

Mid-turn, Acontius' smile dropped as a woman's silky voice rang out coldly.

"Acontius. I was wondering where you were." Artemis approached him, cupping his chin with her cool fingers. "You broke your vow."

Not wholly; it had only been a kiss. But hadn't he done so much worse with the vow? His length ached in need. Every nerve ending crackled to life as he recalled how she'd felt pressing into him, touching, and tasting him.

"Artemis, I can explain." He cast his eyes downward. "I... I..."

"You were lonely and gave in to baser instincts." Artemis curled her lip and shook her head. "You've broken your vow just the same, and you must pay for that." She turned her head toward the hotel, lifting a dark eyebrow. "Or someone must."

"No!" Acontius stilled himself from leaping at her or dropping to his feet to grovel. "Not that. She doesn't know. It isn't her fault I... I screwed up, Artemis."

She said nothing, instead waiting for him to continue. Although he didn't want to, it came spilling out. "Last year, when she was at your temple, I threw an engraved apple at her feet. She read what I wrote: 'I swear by Artemis to marry Acontius.'"

Artemis hissed, releasing his chin as she withdrew. "You..." Her expression fell from fury to disgust. "You dishonor your oath to me in such a way?"

"She doesn't know. I am sorry, I just... I was tired of being alone." Tired of the quiet apartment and the same existence day after day. "She is going back to the states... She doesn't need to be a part of this."

Artemis pursed her lips. She turned her back to him, then laughed. "You are a great fool. If you know she is bound to you, you know the only way to sever that bond is death." She stuck her hand out, summoning her bow, and an arrow appeared in her other hand. "Shall I assist?" They both glowed a warm hue, which illuminated Artemis' pale skin as she nocked the arrow.

Panic lanced through Acontius, and he darted in front of the arrowhead's line of fire. "No! Please, Artemis." He crumpled to the ground at her feet, bowing his head. "You know what it is like to love and lose," he whispered softly. It was a low blow, but he was desperate. Artemis had loved Orion with every fiber of her being, and when he died, she swore an oath never to love again—never to be with anyone else.

Acontius didn't blame her for that. Apollo had plotted against Orion. Seeing him as an unworthy match for his sister, he unleashed a giant scorpion on the skilled hunter. The stealthy creature wound up being the demise of Orion, and in Artemis' misery, she begged her father to set her beloved amongst the stars.

Artemis stilled, but her demeanor grew colder. "You dare use *him* against me?" She lowered her bow, glowering down at him. "I'll grant you leniency, since it was but a kiss, and the girl is ignorant of the situation." As she released the weapons, they dissipated into flecks of gold. "Because of you, that girl will grow sick every time she becomes close to another man, and should she wed them, she'll die." Artemis lifted a finger as Acontius wailed. "I believe that is payment enough, but I'll sweeten the pot for you. If you can earn the heart of that mortal girl, I'll lift your immortality so you may spend a human lifetime with her. But if you cannot gain her love, you'll be a hound for all eternity, and that girl will either be alone for the rest of her life, or die."

Tears stung Acontius' eyes. If he'd known how dire the

circumstance would be, he'd have never acted so impulsively.

Delia wouldn't be in Turkey much longer, just over a week. Could a person fall in love in two weeks' time?

"Thank you, my goddess, for allowing me a chance," he murmured, keeping his head bowed.

"I will see you tomorrow." Artemis walked away without another word, leaving Acontius with his shame, worry, and guilt.

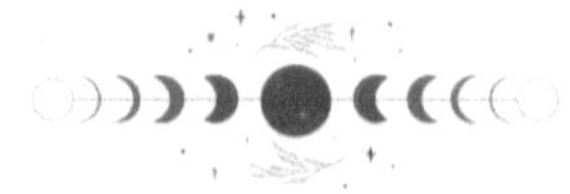

By the first week's end, Acontius had developed a rapid texting relationship with Delia, and when he wasn't at work, they FaceTimed one another, or met halfway in Balıkesir.

Acontius glanced down at his phone, smiling at their rambling texts and recalling their day-trip adventures to the Kaz Mountains and Kazdagi National Park.

Delia: I'm in a small tour group… This guide isn't nearly as fun as you.
Conner: No stories of loyal hound dogs?
Delia: Nope. I'm at the Hippodrome.
Conner: Beware of flying wheels. They hurt when they fly into the stands.
Delia: Hahaha. So funny.

Conner: Ya... miss you too.
Delia: Wish we were hiking again.
Conner: My next day off before you leave for Greece?
Delia: YAS!

He scrolled through to their last conversation before he arrived at the temple.

Conner: Delia, you know I'm not a priest, right?
Delia: OMG. I hope not... I just thought I'd confess a few of my sins... ;)
Conner: You stole a Furby? What even is that?
Delia: Basically a cute demon-possessed furball that talks and moves its eyes.
Conner: That's horrifying... Why are you telling me this and where did you unleash the demon?
Delia: IDK you're easy to talk to. Also, last I saw it was terrorizing Goodwill patrons.
Conner: Only slightly concerning... but tell me more about how easy I am to talk to.
Delia: I can tell you anything, and I feel like you listen and see me for me. You don't judge me. You're kinda perfect so far... I'm waiting for the dream to end.
Conner: LOL far from it, but you're worth listening to.
Delia: FaceTime me after work?
Conner: Always.

As Acontius forced his gaze away from the screen, an intrusive thought entered his mind. The deal with Artemis hung over his head like a guillotine, and while Acontius knew he was supposed to make Delia fall in love, he was the one tumbling head over heels.

Everything about her lit his nerves on fire: her laugh, the light in her dark brown eyes, and her hunger to live.

It hadn't just been a week for him; it had been an entire year. He'd watched her from afar and felt a tug, enough to toss the apple at her feet. And now they were here. Talking, laughing, and sharing those kisses on the beach.

"Acontius." Artemis tore into the turmoil in his mind. "We're opening positions here at the museum. Emin is retiring at the end of the month, and Nihat is leaving for the states next week." She frowned, holding up a stack of papers. "We need more people."

"What positions are open?" He glanced up from his lax position at the front desk. Eyes clouded with boredom, his body hunched over, and his chin propped up with his palm.

Pulling a printed paper from the pile in her arms, she slid it across the desk. "Here."

Acontius scanned the open positions. Over the past few days, he'd learned of Delia's need for a job, something flexible for her health in case it plummeted. And knowing what he knew now... it wouldn't, unless things became serious with another.

"I'll see if I can drum up some interest." Acontius' eyes flicked toward the doorway, where Jonas, one of Artemis' hounds, stood in human form. He was stocky, with dark hair and nearly black eyes. His hair consisted of curls wound tightly against his scalp. In short, he looked the part of a Greek god without the power. He was a servant to a goddess, after all.

"What is he doing here?" Acontius' voice raised an octave.

"We need help, I told you." A smile tugged at Artemis' lips, and she turned away without saying another word to him, leaving Acontius to glare at Jonas.

Jonas was beneath him in every way. He'd also been turned into a hound for attempting to force himself on one of the hunters. Five hundred years as a hound wasn't enough of a punishment in Acontius' mind.

"I'll find better help."

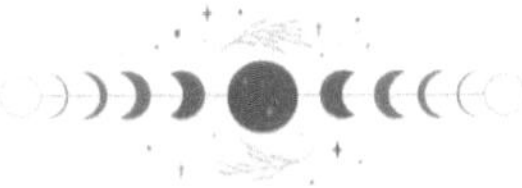

The next day, when Delia FaceTimed him, he brought up the open positions.

"What? You don't want me to leave Turkey?" Delia teased. "I don't know. How often would I have to be in the office? Would I have to move here?" She lowered her voice, leaning closer to the phone. "I don't know how I feel about moving."

Acontius wasn't certain, but he'd have time to ask Artemis. "Send me your resume, and I'll forward it to Arty."

The idea of Delia staying here, living within miles of him, was euphoric, but what did *she* want?

Acontius hoped that a life with him was exactly what she wanted, because then she'd get to live.

"I'll see what I can do, but it wouldn't hurt to send the application to Arty. Besides, I don't want you to leave. Think of the fun we could have in more than two weeks! But I know you have a life in Florida."

She sighed on the other end. "I know." Despite the sigh, she was smiling at him from her hotel bed, surrounded by pillows and her dark hair. "I'll talk to you tomorrow. I've got to get to bed. Another round of sightseeing and eating tomorrow. Sleep tight."

When the call ended, Acontius stared at his Home screen and groaned. What was he doing? Did he actually want Delia working with him, with Jonas and Artemis? Gripping his head, he let out a frustrated growl.

Delia

With only four days left in Turkey, apprehension filled Delia. She frowned, zipping her makeup bag. In a few more days, she would be off to Greece, and then back home too soon after. What she needed to do was make the most of what she had left, knowing Conner didn't hold a place in her future.

She checked her reflection to make sure no mascara was smeared beneath her eye. Gold eyeshadow accented her warm tones, adding more depth to her dark brown eyes. From the days in the sun, her skin was a deeper tan, which complimented the soft yellow blouse she wore.

"I'll call you when I get to Selçuk, Dad. I promise. It's just an interview. I highly doubt I'll land the job considering I live in the states..." If she landed the job, Delia would need to reassess her living situation—or work something out with the museum. That was the entire point of the interview, to see if this would work, and if so, *how.*

Her father walked across the room and hugged her

tightly. "Delia, I have something to say. It's something you brought up a few months ago, about our last trip. I've been thinking about it." He brushed her braid over her back, but as her phone rang, she turned away.

"I'm sorry, Dad! When I get back, we can talk about it." She quickly leaned forward and pressed a kiss to his cheek. Her purse hung on a coat rack, and under it sat a day bag full of clothes and a toothbrush for an overnight stay. She promptly plucked both up and hurried out the door.

In a few hours, she would be with Conner. Butterflies danced away in her belly as she thought of him. It was silly to think it'd only been a week since meeting him, but she felt connected to Conner far more than she ever had with anyone. Being away from him felt strange—like a part of her was being pulled taut.

She bit her bottom lip, smiling broadly as memories from their recent day trip played in her mind.

Conner turned toward her, glancing down at her from on top of the hill. His thumbs hooked into the straps of his backpack as he watched her climb. A broad smile tugged at the corner of his lips as she made it to the peak.

Delia planted her hands on her upper thighs, sucking in deep breaths. It was her brilliant idea to race up the hill. "Gah. Bad idea," she rasped.

"You said you wanted to run it." He shrugged his shoulders and motioned to the view.

"Oh my gods... Look at that." Delia closed the distance between them and leaned against his side. "This... is absolutely beautiful." A breathtaking view of sapphire water

stretched out before them. The mountain range dove into the water, looking more like a god's hand pressing down into the surface than anything. "Thank you for bringing me here."

"Thank you for sharing the moment with me." He dipped his head and kissed her slowly.

Just a fun vacation, she reminded herself. Nothing more. She wasn't ready for more, right? Her fear ramped up. What if this was a start of something serious? What if he, like the others, left her?

Once in the SUV, Delia called Conner and started the long drive down to him. She slid into easy conversation, laughter, and the previous fluttering she'd felt returned tenfold.

Two hours into the drive, the call ended, and a few hours after that, she arrived at Conner's place.

He wrapped his arms around her, spinning her around. "Psychi mou," Conner murmured and leaned in for a kiss.

"Your soul?" Delia's heart leaped at his words, and she met him halfway for a kiss. "You cinnamon roll." She raked her fingers through his hair and smiled. "When am I supposed to be meeting Arty?"

Conner's shoulders slumped "She's already waiting." He lifted a hand to cup the side of her face, his gaze searching hers. "Delia, I have something to talk to you about."

Delia grimaced. "Waiting? That's not nerve-wracking or

anything." She paused, blinking. "Can we talk later? All I'm going to focus on is the interview."

He nodded. "Of course... it can wait. Besides, you'll do fine," he reassured her, and kissed the tip of her nose. Pulling her into his side, Acontius led her to his car. "My shift begins soon. I'll bring you."

And he did. But during the drive, Conner seemed off to Delia, like he was withholding something from her, which seemed odd. What did he have to hide from her? They'd both agreed to let happen whatever may happen.

On arrival at the museum, Conner escorted Delia in, and they parted ways. Arty was supposed to meet her at the front desk and go from there, but she was nowhere to be seen.

Milling around the museum, Delia stopped at an interesting piece: a statue with a broken off nose wearing a robe of animals carved into it. Goat heads peered lifelessly from their place in the headdress, and lions perched on the statue's forearms, while bull testicles hung from where the female figure's breasts would've been. And on the legs of the gown, lions sat stacked on top of goats, which were stacked on top of leopards, and deer. Artemis.

"It's peculiar, isn't it?" a male voice asked from behind her. "How they used to symbolize things back then. This represents so much of our mother goddess. Her nurturing ways, her ability to protect and provide for her people, all wrapped in a statue."

Delia turned her head just enough to inspect the speaker. A museum name tag declared his name was

Jonas. She forced a tense smile and nodded. "I know. Most think those are rows of breasts, but are, in fact, bull testicles. It's believed to symbolize the castrated priests who served her."

The museum employee, allegedly named Jonas, raised his eyebrows and grinned at her. "Well, someone has done her homework."

"I've been here a time or two." She returned her gaze to the statue, hoping the man would go away and leave her until Arty came out. With a hopeful glance, she scanned the area for a woman, but there was no one else, not even Conner.

An uncomfortable feeling crawled up Delia's spine, forcing her to turn and look at the lingering man. "Can I help you?"

He took a step back, clearing his throat. "Sorry. I'm waiting for an interviewee."

Delia's eyes widened. "I'm waiting to meet Arty for an interview..."

"Oh, you must be Delia. You'll be joining me instead. Arty is in a meeting with a few archaeologists. I'm afraid she cannot attend. I'm Jonas, an educator here." A smug expression drew his lips upward into a mockery of a smile.

In her mind, a warning alarm blared. She didn't want to be stuck in a room alone with this man. "I didn't realize educators could interview people," Delia deadpanned.

"When you've worked with the director long enough, you can." Jonas motioned to the hallway.

Reluctantly, Delia followed him down the hall and into

a room set apart from prying eyes. Instinctively, she kept her hand on her keys hanging from her purse as she sat down.

Jonas glanced at the stapled papers in his hand. "I received your resume. Impressive, and we definitely need to refresh our marketing ideas." Jonas sat on the edge of the desk, leaning in toward Delia. "I like these pamphlets you had made for your prior place of employment."

Delia's pulse throbbed in her skull, deafening her.

"So, tell me about yourself."

Delia wetted her lips, trying to focus on the question. "I'm a self-starter, and I enjoy the challenging aspects that the work can often present..." She glanced up at Jonas, and red rushed into her cheeks. The look in his eye told her he didn't care about what she was saying, nor was he listening.

Just as Delia went to stand up, the office door opened. She twisted in the chair to investigate and saw Conner's face. Relief flooded her at once. But why wasn't he with a tour group?

"Arty wants you, Jonas. She's in her office." Conner walked inside, thumbing toward the hallway. Immediately, Jonas' demeanor changed, and the nice guy persona faded.

"How convenient," Jonas spat as he shoved Conner with his shoulder.

Delia's face fell into confusion, but Jonas' sudden attitude change also set her on edge. How dare he snap at Conner! How dare he shove him!

Once Jonas disappeared into the hallway, Delia visibly relaxed. "Thank the gods, I was getting ready to stab him if he got any closer."

"Should've," Conner quipped. He sighed and shook his head. "It's your decision, but I think..."

"If working here means spending alone time with him, I'm out. I don't need this job that badly, and I will not subject myself to that." Confusion rumpled Delia's brow. "Why are you here?"

"When I learned Arty was in a meeting and *he* was going to interview you..." His lips twisted. "You're right to not trust him." Conner paused, leaning down to brush a kiss on the top of her head. "Take my car back to my place, pick me up at five thirty, and we can spend the night together."

Although wasting a few hours in his apartment didn't sound ideal, it would be worth it to grab dinner with him.

Delia stood from the chair. "Do you think he would've hired me?" She tilted her head, and one dark brow lifted in question.

"I imagine so. We need employees. But do you want to work with him?" Conner's lip lifted in disgust.

"No, not really."

"I don't want to work with him either." Conner chuckled and pulled his keys from his pocket. "Make yourself at home. I've got plenty to eat there as well."

Sighing, Delia moved toward him and brushed a kiss to his cheek. "I'll see you later."

A part of her wondered what hidden secrets his apartment held, if any at all. So, with one more parting glance, she left the museum and headed toward his apartment.

The inside, as she'd seen on their FaceTimes, was fairly

simplistic. White walls, no pictures, but tidy. No television, but Delia knew he owned a laptop for work purposes.

A bookshelf as tall as her sat against the wall, crammed with books, mostly on archaeology or history. But there were some gems amongst them, ones that had Delia laughing out loud.

Hitchhiker's Guide to the Galaxy
American Gods
Good Omens

A person's book collection said a lot about them, and this one was rather eclectic. Conner's taste in books were quirky, darker reads.

After milling around his apartment and finding nothing incriminating, Delia plopped down on the couch and took out her phone. She figured she'd better call her father to ease his wild imagination. Otherwise, he'd be calling in reinforcements in no time.

Somehow, her father had come up with over an hour's worth of conversation. Mostly he spent the time discussing opportunities back at home. Her father wanted her to work with him so desperately, and she realized the idea didn't seem so off-putting now.

She was no stranger to work.

Groaning, she reminded herself this was a vacation. Why in Hades' name was she thinking about work, or even trying to apply for a job? "You're an idiot, Delia," she whispered, and curled up on the couch.

Mindless scrolling through the internet it was then.

When five o'clock rolled around, Delia pulled up to the curbside at the museum and hopped over into the passenger seat.

Conner slid into the car and pulled his sports jacket off. His bright hazel eyes bore into Delia, making her insides turn to jelly. He had no right being so beautiful.

"Are you ready for a fun night?"

The way he said it was innocent enough, but Delia wanted more than chaste kisses. She wanted to explore the lean muscles of his body, and although she did want food, she wanted him more.

"We don't have to go out." She leaned forward and placed a soft, lingering kiss to his lips.

He chuckled against her lips, drawing the kiss out in a slow, sensuous dance. "But we do have all night."

"Good point."

"Besides, I have an idea." Conner winked as he drove away from the museum. "One of my favorite places to go when I need to clear my head."

Delia bit her bottom lip, wondering what was on his mind.

In a few minutes, they arrived at Pamucak Beach. People still combed the sand or swam in the sea's warmth. It was still full of life.

Once the car was off, both of them removed their shoes

and headed for the sand. With the sun beginning its descent, Conner wrapped his arm around her waist and focused on it. "This is what I'd like to do every night," he murmured against her temple.

His words, innocent but full of so much emotion, tugged at Delia's heart. She didn't want to leave him behind as just a memory of her trip to Turkey. Twisting away from the view of the sunset, she lifted herself on her toes and kissed him softly.

Conner pulled away, cupping her face. "Delia, I have something to tell you. My name, it's really..."

A crack sounded in the air like a bolt of lightning, but no flash came.

Delia stood stunned, her eyes boring into Conner's, but they weren't on her. They focused on something behind her. As she turned, she realized it wasn't something, but some*one*.

A beautiful woman strode forward, flanked by two canines. She was glaring at Conner and Delia. "Acontius."

Confusion swept through Delia. "Acontius?"

A slow smile spread across the woman's face. "That is his name. The name I gave him, and the name he's had since before the Ottomans stole away pieces of Greece." She bared her teeth as she drew closer. "And he has lied for long enough. You lied to Jonas today, you've been lying to Delia, and you've been lying to me." The air around the woman shuddered. The business suit she wore tore away, like fingers were clawing at it, shredding it until bare skin appeared. However, in place of the vanishing fabric, ivory cloth appeared until the woman stood in a shortened chiton. She looked like a Greek goddess come to life.

Was this some kind of trick? Delia frowned.

None of the beachgoers seemed to notice the magic act. No one even glanced in their direction.

"Artemis, no. I still have time left."

"Oh, you do. But you've lied to me, and I am not keen on liars." She flexed her hand, fingers pointing toward the hounds at her feet.

Delia pulled away from Conner, eyeing the woman incredulously. "What is going on?"

A bow materialized in the woman's hands. Artemis, her name was Artemis. As in the goddess?

"Acontius, why don't you finally spout some truth?" The hounds at Artemis' feet sprung to life, lips curled and teeth bared as they stalked forward.

Stepping backward, Delia looked to Conner in panic. "What... what?" He'd lied to her? It wasn't as if this "truth" were believable, and despite what her eyes showed her, Delia wasn't sure what she was seeing was even real.

"Delia, I... my name *is* Acontius."

EIGHT

Acontius

As the hounds crept closer, Acontius extended his arm and pushed Delia behind him. This wasn't how he'd planned on revealing the truth to her.

Artemis pulled the strands of the glamor tighter, shielding them from the people at the beach, hiding them in plain sight. After centuries with the goddess, and receiving her blessing when he was an infant, Acontius could feel the construction of the glamor.

She could end Acontius' life, and none would be the wiser.

"I have... much to tell you. I am not mortal. I am one of Artemis' hunters, sworn to remain pure and serve her. She once saved my life, and I was granted immortality."

Delia gaped at him, lifting a shaking hand to her lips. "W-what? Are you kidding me?" Her voice climbed in pitch, breaking at the end. "This isn't real. This can't actually be happening."

"Oh, it is. I assure you," said Artemis. "I don't know

what game he is playing, but he belongs to me and can never be yours." She held her bow upright, tilting her head as she nocked it. "Acontius, say goodbye to this form."

"No. We made a deal, Artemis. Are you saying you lied to me?" Acontius stepped forward, ignoring the posturing dogs at his sides. One of them was Jonas, and the other some wretched human who'd lost himself along the way. "You are not a villain. Don't do this. You are a goddess, and you are just. I..." He tore his eyes away from her swirling silver pair. "I wanted a chance at an actual life! I never... I never had a choice. You cannot in honesty say that I had one, can you?"

Artemis faltered for a moment.

Acontius had been a boy, a foolish, eight-year-old boy, when he'd chosen this life. Had he truly been old enough to dedicate himself in such a manner?

"You decided."

"I was a child! I wanted to make you proud, and you were the closest I had to a mother."

Artemis' scowl disappeared, her expression sliding into an unreadable expression. But she did lower her bow, and the hounds retreated to her side.

Acontius' chest rose and fell quickly. The air was thick with tension, and so quiet that the soft intake of breath from behind him told him Delia was still there, and she was crying.

"This isn't real, this can't be..." Delia murmured over and over.

His heart pounded so hard, he thought it would leap

from his chest and cease. Still, Artemis hadn't mentioned a word about the deal, which surprised him.

Artemis' fingers relinquished the hold on her bow and arrow, which vanished before they hit the ground. Closing the distance between herself and Acontius, she grabbed ahold of his shirt. "You have two days before I return, and that is all."

The surrounding air shuddered as the landscape sunk inward, then expanded. In a blink, the beach was in motion again, as if nothing had happened. Artemis was gone, and so were the hounds.

"Delia," Acontius turned around to face her. She held her shaking hands over her mouth, and with every step he took forward, she took another backward.

"No! What was that?" Delia shrieked, motioning to the space where Artemis once was. "Let me at least try to process this." After a few moments, she started walking toward the car again.

Muttering a curse under his breath, Acontius followed her. "Delia..."

"Still processing. Was everything you told me a lie?" She spat out, huffing through the effort of walking in the sand.

"No. None of it was. I never lied to you! My family is from Kea. I've omitted truths, but everything..." Acontius snagged her elbow, halting her in her tracks. "It's all true. Please, Delia... please." He glanced off to the side, willing the earth to open up and for Hades to drag him to the depths, away from his misery. "I love you."

She sucked a breath in and reeled back, like someone slapped her. "Don't say that."

"I know. You're leaving, and it's foolish to try." His hold on her elbow weakened until he released her. Defeat etched itself onto his face, and he felt every year tacked onto his body. As fast as his heart had pounded before, he was fairly certain it was shattering now. "I'll bring you back."

Delia said nothing. Not as they got to the car, not as she sat in the passenger seat, and not before she drove away from his apartment in her own rental, leaving Acontius to wallow in misery.

If he'd only listened to Artemis, if he'd stayed true to the vow, this never would have happened. "Damn it all." He pounded his fist against the side of his apartment complex, his eyes wrenching shut. Every piece of him ached. What an idiot he'd been.

With two days left until Artemis came to make good on her promise, Acontius was desperate, and the only thing he could think to do was to drag another individual into this horrendous mess.

Racing across the street, he darted into the convenience store and scoured the shelves for a sleeping aid. When he found a few, he scooped them up and ran to the checkout line.

The clerk raised an eyebrow but said nothing as he slipped the products into a bag.

Not waiting until he was in the comfort of his apartment, Acontius opened the package of melatonin outside of the store and downed a handful of the gummies.

In hopes of quickening the drowsiness, he ran across the street, jogged up a few flights of stairs, and then finally burst into his apartment. With his blood pumping quicker, it was only a matter of time before sleep tugged at him.

Acontius sunk onto his couch, frustrated and out of breath. "Morpheus, I know you hear me. I need to speak with you." Nothing happened, not yet. Not until the last tendrils of sleep pulled Acontius under.

After fifteen minutes, his eyes grew heavier, and his breathing slowed. "Morpheus," Acontius slurred, slumping over onto the couch in a heap.

Blackness met him. The sound of the light humming in his apartment faded away, until all he heard was the soft *tip-tap* of bare feet. The tickling sensation of a feather dragging on Acontius' hand roused him.

Blinking away the sleep, Acontius sat up, eyes focusing on the man who crouched before him. A pair of intense blue eyes watched him carefully, and long, dark, wavy hair framed a stern face.

The apartment still looked the same, except the edges held a wavering light, as if the image of the room would peel away at any moment. This wasn't real; it was Morpheus' realm.

"Why do you call me?" Black eyebrows furrowed in question as he leaned in, pushing his forefinger into Acontius' chest. "You are one of Artemis' hunters." It wasn't a question. The male stood to his full height, clucking his tongue as he spun away. "I won't interfere with her business."

"Wait! It isn't. I need… I need a favor. It's for a mortal."

Morpheus halted, turning on his heel, his black feathered wings tucked close to his body. A flowy, button-up shirt revealed the hardened tan flesh beneath. "What price are you willing to pay for my services?"

Of course he'd want payment. Nothing came without a price, especially from a god. "A dream. One I've kept for centuries."

Folding his arms, Morpheus waited patiently. "Which is?"

"The dream of my mother."

Surprise registered on Morpheus' face. "The very dream that Artemis gifted you?"

Irritation crept into Acontius. He sat up from the floor of his apartment and strode forward. "A dream won't bring her back or change the course of history. But what it can do is change the course of my future."

Nodding, Morpheus' posture relaxed, and he extended his hand. "Fair enough, child. What is it you want?"

"Weave a dream for Delia Rentumis with an apology from me, but also the truth. My truth, and what could be for us."

"That is dangerous, Acontius," Morpheus hissed. "Showing a mortal their future is beyond foolish."

"I *am* a fool."

Morpheus snorted. "This is apparent."

Desperate for Morpheus to do this favor, Acontius pressed on. "If she doesn't see, then she will die. If she marries anyone but me, she will die, and it'll be my fault. I cannot bear that for an eternity, not even as a hound."

Morpheus seemed to weigh his words, then sighed, motioning for him to step forward. "Come closer."

Acontius stepped forward, closing his eyes. He remembered what it had felt like when the memory seeped into his skull: warm and comforting. But this time, something would be removed.

A bright, flickering light danced in front of him as Morpheus' hand drew closer to Acontius' temple, and when his cool touch connected with his skin, his head throbbed. A minor inconvenience, like brain freeze from ice cream, and in a split second, it was gone.

Acontius attempted to conjure up the memory of his mother.

Gone.

Her face gone, her laugh gone.

Gone.

"It is done. Although, I cannot say what outcome she'll choose, because the future is a spider web of choices. I make no promises to you as to what will come of this, Acontius." Morpheus paused, twisting his lips. "What was Artemis going to do?"

Pinching the bridge of his nose, Acontius sighed. "Turn me into a hound and let my stupid vow be the end of Delia. In turn, I'd live with my idiotic consequences for as long as she allowed me to live."

Nodding, Morpheus picked at his nails. "Fitting. It never fails to surprise me."

"What?"

"Desperation in mortals. It drives them to do the most mindless things." Morpheus rolled his eyes and began to walk away. "I'll weave the dream for you, child, but I make no promises it'll work. And should this earn more of Artemis' wrath, I'll not be involved."

"Thank you. I am in your debt." Dangerous words.

"No. We are even. I have your dream, and you have my word. Do not bargain for more. Now, sleep deep and sleep well."

Morpheus' figure blurred as Acontius fell deeper into sleep, until his mind knew no more.

NINE

Delia

W as this what it felt like to have a mental breakdown? The more Delia tried to process the evening's turn of events, the more she thought she was losing it.

The gods were real.

As a girl, she'd always believed they were, but now, as a full-grown adult? It was like believing in a fairytale, yet here she was.

Conner—no, Acontius—was a figure from history. Like this was some kind of Greek retelling of *Kate and Leopold*. Wiping tears from her eyes, she focused on the roadway. "No, this is real life. And even if I did love him... This is stupid."

It didn't matter. In two days' time, she'd be gone, and her vacation would come to an end. This brief respite from reality would be over. She just needed to keep herself collected so her father didn't wag his finger and tell her, "*I told you so.*"

Of course, he'd remind her she was still reeling from heartbreak, that she needed time to heal, and he was right. But it had felt good, natural, and the way she'd clicked with Conner—Acontius—felt like fate.

After a long, miserable car ride to Istanbul, Delia burst through the hotel door and found her father reading in the living room space. He frowned at her and motioned to a chair.

At one in the morning, he should've been fast asleep, but he wasn't, and it struck Delia as odd.

"I know. You were right, it was stupid. I shouldn't have rushed in, and now it hurts... again." She gripped at her chest, wishing that she could mend the shattering pieces, and sat down. "I'm so stupid." Her heart ached beneath her hand. Sure, it beat steadily, but with every pulse, it hurt. Wanting. Needing.

"No. You're going to listen to me. It's about that boy. It took me a bit, but I recognize him from last year. He and I spoke at length about the Temple of Artemis." Her dad's bushy brows knit together as he closed the book he was reading. "You were so eager to leave before I had a chance to speak to you, and on the phone... it didn't seem right. Delia, remember last year? The engraved apple you found and told me about?"

As the question registered in her head, Delia threw her hands up. What did that have to do with... Her thoughts collided as she wracked her brain, trying to remember the inscription. She blinked, vaguely recalling her father walking away from one of the tour guides last year, smiling and joking about how *he* should be an educator for the museum. "Yeah?" she asked shakily.

"Since we've been here, I've done some prodding myself. You uttered those words on sacred ground, binding you to this... Acontius. You swore to the goddess herself that you would. What happens when you don't hold up your end? Delia, this could be why you're getting sick."

Up until today, Delia would've laughed at him for suggesting Artemis was real, let alone this Acontius figure. But Conner *was* him. That meant he'd seen her last year, and he hadn't mentioned it at all in the past two weeks? Not to mention that the gods were still alive and well—that was a big detail he'd left out. Her skin cooled, and she felt light-headed.

"This can't be happening."

"I've always believed they were among us. No one crafts temples for myths. No one has cult followings if they're not real, but this proves it. Is... is Conner's name Acontius?" He wetted his lips, leaning forward, a feverish look entering his gaze. "I thought it strange the way he looked at you when you first met. Like a lovesick pup, but if he's the one... it makes sense."

"Dad, they are very much real, and they are *here*." Delia's voice wavered as she lifted her hands to her face. "I saw her. I saw Artemis. She had her bow and she... she was so angry."

Her father leaped from the couch, hands on his head as he paced the room with a newfound energy. He looked torn between excitement and nervousness. How often did someone get to see a god or goddess face to face?

"Tell me everything."

So she did. She told him of what little she knew, and what had transpired on the beach.

"Oh. That is strange. Artemis only ever took on females in her order. I wonder what made him so special?"

Delia didn't know; she hadn't stuck around to find out. She'd run as fast and far away from him as she could get. "I don't know, Dad. His ability to keep secrets?"

Her father tsked. "Would you have believed him? You can barely believe it now, let alone last week when you didn't know him." He looked torn, not that Delia blamed him. Without a doubt, she knew he wanted to console her and also use the moment as a teachable one.

Delia didn't want a life lesson. She wanted direction.

"And what now? I'm bound to a man I don't know? Destined to be sick for the rest of my life if I don't marry him?" She stood from the chair, flinging her hands up over her head in frustration.

It wasn't fair.

But then, life wasn't fair.

Her father frowned as he approached her, gripping her biceps. "My dear, all I can say is that in two weeks, I saw a new life enter you. I saw you happier than I've ever seen you. Whether that's due to being here or with him, only you know the answer. Tomorrow, as much as you don't want to... you'll need to call him to get answers."

She didn't want to. Not after she'd left Acontius without

so much as a word. Delia winced as she thought about it. She *had* said something to him, but it had been, "Don't say that" when he admitted he loved her.

"I don't think I can do that." She shook her head, running her hands over her face. "I... need to go to bed. I'm exhausted after the drive, and I just don't want to be awake."

"All right, get some rest." Her father wrapped his arms around her, hugging her tightly before kissing her cheek. "We will figure this out."

Delia wasn't so sure.

Not bothering to check her phone, Delia changed into her pajamas and settled into bed. Sleep came faster than she thought it would.

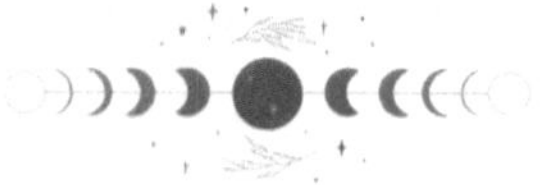

Soft tendrils of light peeked through the window into Delia's room. It felt as though she'd just fallen asleep, and now the sun was waking her? She groaned and turned her back to the window, but the light grew stronger.

I made a promise that I aim to keep.

A man's voice rumbled through the room, startling Delia awake. In the corner of her room, a tall, beautiful man unfolded from the chair and strode forward, massive black wings outstretched, reaching each opposite wall.

"It's time to understand," he breathed, folding his wings back in as he sat on the bed. "Do not be afraid, Delia."

And for some odd reason, she wasn't. A soothing feeling spread through her as his fingers stroked her temple. "Enjoy your dream. I promise to give you rest after this. It'll be tiring."

After a soft kiss to her lips, Morpheus pulled away, chuckling.

Perplexed with the direction the dream was taking, Delia sat up, trying to reach for the angel man, but her body collapsed to the bed and her head grew dizzy.

Image after image flashed in her mind. An infant swaddled in cloth. A boy standing before Artemis' temple. Acontius growing into himself. His truth, his life, flashed before her eyes.

Delia thrashed, not wanting to see anymore, but then she saw herself through his eyes the first time he saw her. It was strange seeing herself look so *lonely*. She wore a smile, but it was empty. Then she glanced up and saw Acontius. Delia had seen him last year? Why didn't she remember?

As if her heart weren't already throbbing enough, the dream allowed her to feel his desolation, his empathy toward her in that moment, and she watched as he decided to write on the apple, sealing their fate. An immense, overwhelming desire to start anew and truly experience life bloomed within her, but she realized it wasn't her emotion—it was Acontius'.

By the end of the visions, Delia had been reduced to

tears. "Please, no more. Let me wake, please." But relief wouldn't come any time soon.

Instead of seeing what had been, Delia saw herself in Florida again, only she wasn't alone. She sat at the beach, fingers laced with a familiar set of digits. Acontius. In another flash, she saw him again, and he was looking at her with a nervous smile. Another image brought her to her wedding day, and as the point of view changed, she saw Acontius staring down at her.

All of it came crashing to an end, plunging her into a deep darkness. Confusion swept through her, clouding her thoughts, and she knew no more as exhaustion took control, pulling her into a restful slumber.

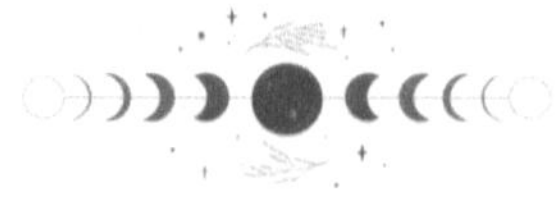

Delia startled awake. She fumbled for her phone, half asleep, and lifted it.

No missed calls.

Why would he try to call? She'd given him no reason. But as the screen came into focus, she saw that it was nearly three o'clock in the afternoon. Her father had let her sleep that late? Tossing the covers back, she rushed out of bed and dialed Acontius.

No answer.

She left him a message: "I know we didn't leave on good

terms, but please call me as soon as you can." She hung up, chewing on her bottom lip as she mentally fussed over last night. Those dreams... That hadn't been an angel last night, it couldn't have been. Mentally, she ticked off her knowledge of Greek mythology—or history, since it clearly wasn't a myth. "Morpheus?" she squeaked. The God of Dreams had visited her? Kissed her, even. "Hey, Dad?" Delia called as she walked into the living area. "Dad?" She frowned when he didn't answer, but as she walked to the table and saw a note, she sighed.

Pumpkin,
I let you sleep in. The first two attempts to wake you didn't
work. You had a rough night, so I figured you needed sleep.
I'm returning our rental since we leave tomorrow evening for
Greece.
Don't forget to eat.
XX
Dad

No. No. No. No.
    No.
No car meant no speeding down to Selçuk and apologizing to Acontius. It meant not being able to see his face or sort through her horrendous sea of feelings. This was all too much to process, and yet she was being forced to.

Delia tried calling Acontius again. "Please answer..."

No answer.

At the risk of coming across as unstable, she called him again. This time, someone picked up.

"Hello?" a groggy Acontius answered.

Temporary relief flooded through her. "Oh, thank the gods." She drew in a deep breath and threw caution to the wind. "Can you get here tonight? I know it's late, but my dad returned the car, and I can't get down there, and I really need to see you in person."

It sounded like he was rummaging through a cabinet, like small bottles clanging against the counter, then a string of curses sprung forth—some swears Delia knew and others she didn't.

"What is it?"

"It's three already?" Acontius swore again. "I'll be there. Delia, I need to talk to you about a lot more than just what happened. I'm sorry. More sorry than you know. But I have to hang up... I need to contact someone."

Delia blinked. Whatever conversation she expected to have, it wasn't this one. She frowned. "Okay. We'll talk, but I leave tomorrow at two."

"I know."

Acontius

Morpheus held true to his word as Acontius knew he would.

It was late, and it would be pushing the time constraint to its limit if he drove to Istanbul.

He needed speed, and more than that, he needed...

The sound of glass shattering in the kitchen broke through Acontius' thoughts. He peeled back his blankets and jogged into the living room, then toward the small kitchen. Nothing was there except a shattered vase.

"Morpheus told me you were sticking it to Artemis," a voice rang out from behind him. "Can I help rile her up?"

As Acontius turned to face the speaker, he wasn't surprised to find a head of sandy brown curls and dark, mischievous eyes peering back at him.

"Hermes."

Hermes stroked a hand down his trimmed beard and leaned forward. "Artemis, though lovely, has quite a temper, much like her twin. The plight of your mortal girl hasn't fallen on deaf ears. We all agree you're an idiot, but she doesn't deserve to suffer." He paused for a moment, then reached out and placed his hand on Acontius' shoulder. "You will owe me nothing for this."

"For wh–" Mid-sentence, Hermes pulled him in for what he assumed was a hug, but instead of meeting a firm chest, he met air. Air that had no substance, no ground beneath it, no sky above. Hermes had pushed him through a portal, away from his apartment and into... where?

Acontius wasn't new to traveling through a portal. He'd gone through several with Artemis, but this was too fast, dizzying even. Instead of a smooth transition, this one was rushed and choppy, like falling and hitting every branch on the way down. It didn't hurt, but by the end of it, he didn't know which way was up and which was down.

Abruptly, the traveling stopped, and Acontius' face connected with marble flooring. He swore and slowly propped himself up. The sound of footsteps caught his attention, and his eyes found a pair of bare feet. But it was the surprised gasp and choked sob that punched his gut.

"Co...Acontius? Oh my god." Delia rushed forward, her hands cupping his face tenderly as she gazed down at him. "H...How are you here?"

He swayed, holding his stomach as he fought back the nausea from the rough trip. "Give me a second." Once he gathered his wits, his shoulders sagged. "Hermes."

Delia's eyes widened. "Hermes?"

Acontius didn't want to talk about Hermes, as thankful as he was for his meddling. He wanted to speak to Delia;

time was running out. "Delia I..." Acontius started, then looked around the room, half expecting Hermes to stroll out.

"I'm sorry," she interjected. "I didn't know... and this is a lot to take in."

"I wish there had been an easier way. It wasn't like I could open up and say I was one of Artemis' hunters... You'd have written me off and likely suggested I seek help, right?" He smiled wryly, lifting his hands to grab her wrists gently. "Don't answer that," he teased softly. "Listen, we have no time to waste. Artemis will come for me. I... we struck a deal. I tried to buy us more time, but I think I made things worse." He sucked his bottom lip into his mouth. What he'd wanted was for Delia to have an out from the vow, but he'd only tangled the situation further.

"What? Acontius, I know about the apple."

His name on her lips sent a thrill through him, and he wanted to hear her say it again. "That isn't it. If by midnight I haven't captured your heart, I'll be cursed as a hound for eternity, and you can never marry, or if you do, your health will diminish rapidly." Acontius frowned. "I never meant for any of this..."

Delia sucked in a breath and pressed her forehead against his. "People do asinine things when they're in love." She released her hold on his face and sunk to the floor, shaking her head. "In two weeks, I've fallen head over heels in love with you." She looked up at the ceiling with tears pooling in her eyes, then in a steady stream, they trailed down her cheeks. "When I left Florida, I wanted to heal and leave my worries behind, but what I found here was you. I found life, and through that, I discovered myself too."

Acontius let her speak, all the while, his heart hammered in his chest. He was afraid to breathe, wondering if this was perhaps another dream of Morpheus'.

"I should have told you at the beach. I love you. You should have told me the truth, but maybe this was how it was all supposed to work out."

"Fate." Acontius released a breath, his hands cupping her cheeks tenderly. "I've waited centuries to feel this way about someone. Centuries. Never in all of my lifetimes has someone ensnared me body and soul."

Light pooled into the room, crackling with a familiar energy. Artemis. In a quick movement, Acontius shielded Delia from view. He rolled up to his knee, ready to face his goddess if he must.

"Acontius, you enlisted the help of not one but two gods against me." Artemis ground her words out, seething. The chiton she wore billowed in a wind that wasn't present, but the energy and fury radiated from her. "Why should I honor my deal if you gained aid?"

"Because you never said I couldn't receive aid. More than that, I've succeeded."

Fury flashed in Artemis' silver gaze. She strode forward, eyeing the two of them.

"I love him. Weren't those the terms of your agreement?" Delia blurted. "I love him."

Artemis flinched. Her lips pursed as she visibly considered

the information, clenching her fists by her side. "Very well. I'll honor our terms. But know this, Delia Rentumis: should you not marry him, you'll never be in a relationship henceforth."

"I know," Delia murmured.

"Acontius, you have served me faithfully until now, and you have been akin to a son to me, whether I've shown it or not. I wish you happiness, and you have my blessing." Artemis nodded to him, smiling. "I release you from your service, and by doing so, I strip you of your immortality." Artemis stretched her arm out, her fingers closed into a fist as if she were drawing a piece of him out. "Know that the storm brewing will touch you now."

Apollo. She meant Apollo's plague.

Acontius stood, unsure of his next move. Then, falling back on a very human sentiment, he rushed forward to embrace Artemis. The only mother he'd ever known. The one who raised him. "Thank you for everything. For the gift of life, motherhood, and so much more, Artemis."

She stiffened beneath his touch, but then relaxed. "Be well. And also you, Delia. A storm brews on the horizon. Be prepared." The last of her words faded as her image rippled. One moment she stood there, and the next, Artemis was gone.

Bone weary, Acontius dropped to his knees, nearly sobbing. Delia approached him from behind and rubbed his back, her arm slipping over his shoulder.

"I never meant..."

"I know..." Delia's lips pressed soft kisses against his

cheek. "I didn't either, but we both did. Let's forget what we've done and make our own way."

Their own way... Acontius liked the sound of that. "To Greece it is, then?"

Delia laughed. "Our own way... In Greece, laying on the beach, watching the sunset."

That sounded lovely and perfect, but there was something he needed to get off his chest first. "Yes, but I have to tell you something. It's about Apollo, and it's going to affect us all..."

ACKNOWLEDGMENTS

Thank you for reading Acontius and Delia's story. This is actually based off of the greek story Acontius & Cydippe. A tale about a beautiful male who saw a young noblewoman and was enamored by her. Who says love at first sight isn't real? I decided to rename Cydippe for obvious reasons, and it didn't fit with a modern girl's name. In the original story, this all took place at a festival in Delos–hence me picking Delia, which means, "born on the island of Delos."

I actually did a lot of research for this! I took my liberties of course, because it's fantasy! But it was fun to research locations and actually realizing that Artemis' temple is in modern day Turkey was pretty cool!

The deeper I dove into the geography and history of this story, the more I realized I wanted to expand on the stories within. So... if you've made it this far... Stay tuned, because Artemis, Apollo, Morpheus...and a whole lot of other characters will be making an appearance in more stories.

A huge shout out to Candace Robinson for helping me out and beta reading it! You're a gem and I don't know where I'd be without you.

Thank you Meg Dailey for agreeing to take this little nugget on and editing it. Without you...it wouldn't be polished and it certainly wouldn't be pretty!

An on-going thank you to my new and old readers/reviewers. Without you, I wouldn't have the heart to continue writing.

Thank you, Tanya for listening to me meltdown on occasion when I think I should throw in the towel, and again thank you for beating it out of me.

A massive sloppy kiss to Lou Wilham and Christis Christie, who are always there for me no matter what. My original writing crew, shoulders to lean on, and ears who listen to help me hammer out some details.

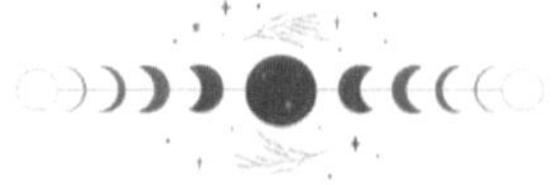

ABOUT ELLE BEAUMONT

 Elle Beaumont is a writer who loves creating vivid fantasy and science fiction worlds in the young adult genre as well as new adult. She lives in south-eastern Massachusetts with her husband and two children. When not writing or chasing around her children she can be seen crocheting, candle-making and taking care of her animals. More than once she has proclaimed that coffee is life blood and it is how she refrains from becoming a zombie

For more information visit www.ellebeaumontbooks.com Or follow Elle on social media!

facebook.com/ellebeaumontbooks

twitter.com/ellebeaumont

instagram.com/ellebeaumontbooks

pinterest.com/ellebeaumontbooks

bookbub.com/authors/elle-beaumont

amazon.com/Elle-Beaumont

STREET TEAM

If you enjoyed this story and would love to connect with like minded individuals, you may want to consider joining the street team.

What does it have to offer?

- Acceptance into an exclusive Facebook group to share your thoughts, talk to Elle, and engage with other fans
- Access to Street Team only giveaways
- Access to early copies of Elle's unpublished work.
- Exclusive Q&A sessions or live "hangouts"
- Ability to vote on bonus content, next release, and more!

Does that sound like something you'd be interested in?
facebook.com/groups/ElleBeaumontStreetTeam

THE OFFICIAL PLAYLIST

You can find the complete "Apple of Fate" playlist on Spotify by searching for Elle Beaumont.

1. Lost and Found by Katie Herzig
2. Perfect by The Piano Guys
3. Something Just Like This by The Chainsmokers ft. Coldplay
4. Waiting for Superman by Daughtry
5. Let's Hurt Tonight by OneRepublic
6. Forgive Me Friend by Smith & Thell ft. Swedish Jam Factory
7. No Vacancy by OneRepublic
8. Can't Let Go by Faydee
9. Good Years by Zayn
10. Under The Stars by Charmes ft. Andres Sierra

Of the Deep

Blood from a Stone

Something in the Shadows

Link by Link

Veiled Allurement

Die From A Broken Heart

The Dragon's Bride

The Castle of Thorns (November '21)

Seeds of Sorrow (2022)

The Dragon's Thorn (2022)

The Medusa Project by Lou Wilham

Everyone takes things that don't belong to them.

From Medusa, it was her reputation. From Poseidon, it was his freedom.

When Poseidon is released from prison, after years of being locked away, the bodies start piling up, and all fingers point to Medusa. Agent Kyrie Alcide of the Perseus Initiative is tasked with investigating the case, and keeping tabs on Medusa. But Kyrie is about to find out that everything in the legend of the infamous gorgon might not be as it seems.

Now, if Kyrie can't discover who the real murderer is Medusa could find herself their next victim.

Available Now

Clouded by Envy by Candace Robinson

Sometimes the very thing you wish for, is your undoing...

Brenik has always been envious of his twin sister, Bray. Everything always came naturally to Bray, even after crossing through a portal from their fae world, while Brenik spent his time in her shadow. So, when Brenik discovers a way to get what he has always desired--to become human-- he takes it. However, the gift turns out to be a curse that alters him in ways he never saw coming.

Bray can't help but be concerned for her brother, more so when he vanishes. While waiting for Brenik to return, she meets two brothers who realize she is not the least bit human. Her dark bat-like wings are proof of that. But some-how, an aching bond forms between Bray and the older brother, Wes.

When Bray reunites with Brenik, she finds an overpowering need for blood stirring deep within him. If Bray doesn't help Brenik put an end to his curse, it will not only damage those who get close to him, but it could also destroy whatever is blooming between her and Wes.

Available Now

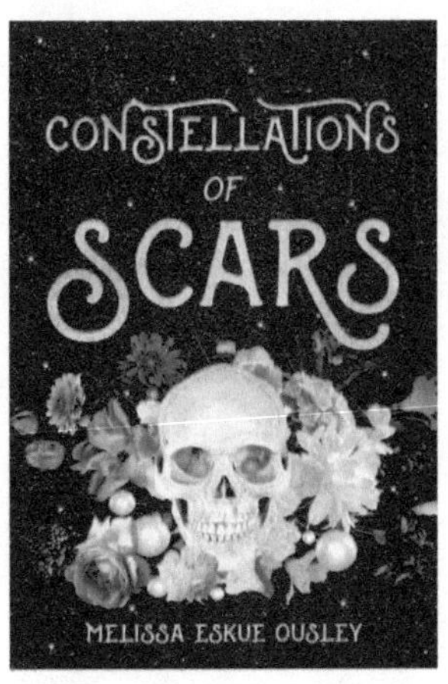

Constellations of Scars by Melissa Eskue Ousley

Not all gifts are a blessing. Some are a curse.

When Amelia turned 12, she began growing pearls. Every month, a crop of beautiful pearls bursts from the skin on her back. Her mother, Denise, believes her daughter is blessed, and sells the pearls to put food on the table. Amelia sees her condition as a curse. As the pearls form, her body aches and her skin grows feverish. The harvest of pearls brings temporary relief from the pain, but leaves her back marred by scars. Denise hides Amelia away from the world, worried that Amelia's gift will be discovered and she will be abducted for the wealth she can provide.

Now a young woman, Amelia realizes she has become her mother's captive, and plans her escape. When she runs away from home, she finds a new family in a troupe of performers at a museum of human oddities. She soon discovers the world is much more dangerous than her mother feared.

Available Now